"Jeremy? I'm here!"

Only it didn't make sense, because her voice seemed to come from somewhere far below him.

"Keep calling!" he yelled.

Slowly, he crept toward the cliff edge, trying not to make too much noise with his boots for fear of drowning out her calls, all the while thinking angry thoughts. *What a party, huh?* he wanted to ask. *Aren't you glad you brought cupcakes for this?* To say those things would be cruel, but it didn't stop him from thinking them. Not even Jeremy Moon, professional risk assessor, could be rational all the time.

"Jeremy?" Whitney called again. She sounded closer. But he still couldn't see her. Unless...

He edged forward, his every step sending cascades of rocks spilling below. He could see them roll, roll and then disappear over the drop-off. He eased forward until he could see over the edge.

Whitney was at the bottom of the cliff...

Jennifer Brown is the award-winning author of young adult and middle-grade novels, including *Perfect Escape*, *Thousand Words*, *Torn Away* and the Shade Me series. Her acclaimed debut novel, *Hate List*, was selected as an ALA Best Book for Young Adults, a *VOYA* "Perfect Ten" and a *School Library Journal* Best Book of the Year, and her novel *Bitter End* was a 2012 YALSA Best Fiction for Young Adults. Her debut middle-grade novel, *Life on Mars*, was the winner of the 2017 William Allen White Children's Book Award.

Jennifer is also the nationally bestselling author of several women's fiction novels under the pseudonym Jennifer Scott. She lives in Kansas City, Missouri. Visit her at jenniferbrownauthor.com.

Peril at
the Peak

JENNIFER BROWN

LOVE INSPIRED
INSPIRATIONAL ROMANCE

LOVE INSPIRED®
INSPIRATIONAL ROMANCE

Recycling programs
for this product may
not exist in your area.

ISBN-13: 978-1-335-42701-4

Peril at the Peak

Copyright © 2021 by Jennifer Brown

All rights reserved. No part of this book may be used or reproduced in
any manner whatsoever without written permission except in the case of
brief quotations embodied in critical articles and reviews.

This is a work of fiction. Names, characters, places and incidents are either the
product of the author's imagination or are used fictitiously. Any resemblance
to actual persons, living or dead, businesses, companies, events or locales is
entirely coincidental.

This edition published by arrangement with Harlequin Books S.A.

For questions and comments about the quality of this book, please contact us
at CustomerService@Harlequin.com.

Love Inspired
22 Adelaide St. West, 40th Floor
Toronto, Ontario M5H 4E3, Canada
www.Harlequin.com

Printed in U.S.A.

I sought the Lord, and he heard me
and delivered me from all my fears.
—*Psalm* 34:4

For Scott, always.

Acknowledgments

While nearly all of my books in some way touch on the theme of connection, this book is the first opportunity that I've had to more fully explore the connection between the human and the Divine. Could we ever possibly muster the bravery that it takes to reach each other if it weren't for our connection with God to strengthen our grip?

I consider every book that I write to be the result of a granting of prayers, and this one to be a granting of many years of prayers. The people who've taken this journey with me are also answers to those prayers.

First and foremost, thank you to my agent, Cori Deyoe, for always being willing to hike to the peak with me and for carrying the water bottles and the granola bars and not getting mad when I leave my backpack behind.

Thank you to everyone on the Love Inspired team who worked to make this book the best that it can be, especially my editor, Johanna Raisanen, whose positivity and enthusiasm are unmatched and so contagious. In some ways, editing a book must be a little like wandering a mountain forest in a storm, confident that the path is there to be found and that, together, we will reach it.

Special thanks to Zoya Shepherd for the striking cover.

Thank you to my family, for always waiting for me at the peak with the cupcakes, even if it takes me quite some time to get there. You are my jubilant rescue flares and I love you most.

Finally, thank you to God for listening and answering and, of course, for sending the woodpeckers.

Chapter One

Whitney sat up with a gasp, seeing nothing but the darkness behind her sleep mask. In her dream, her mother was knocking at the back door, having brought Whitney's favorite traditional birthday lemon cheesecake. But as sleep sloughed away, her heart slowed, and she became more aware of her surroundings. She realized that the lemon cheesecake was just a dream. As was the image of her sweet mother.

But the knocking was very real, and there it was again. Definitely coming from the back door. It was barely dawn. Since it couldn't be her mother knocking... Well, then, who could it be at this hour? And why wouldn't they come to the front door?

She shucked off her sleep mask and tossed it onto the pillow, then slowly, as if sneaking up on someone, slithered out of bed. The bay window in her bedroom allowed an unobstructed view of the back door if she peeked just right.

She tiptoed to the window, slid aside the curtain,

and squinted into the gray light of morning. But there was nobody there.

Wait. Not nobody. A bird. Black-and-white body. Red crown. Perching on the doorknob, its little head poking forward and striking the wood in a blur. A blur that just happened to match the weird—and now that Whitney thought about it, inhumanly fast—knocking sound.

A woodpecker?

She'd never seen one in real life, which was strange for someone living in Southern Missouri. Woodpeckers were common here, and if she were looking, she'd quite likely have seen many. But she wasn't, and she hadn't. And she'd certainly never heard of one pecking at someone's back door, as if asking to come in for a cup of tea. Was that even a thing?

"I have a feeling you're behind this, Mom." She said this to the ceiling, a new habit she'd formed since her mother's passing. "A woodpecker for my thirtieth birthday? Funny gift idea, but I would have rather had the cheesecake."

Then, in spite of herself, she cracked up. Because it was a little funny, thinking she was being awakened by some bogeyman, only to find a three-ounce bird.

"He does look like he's wearing a little red feather birthday hat, though," she said, which reminded her that she needed to pack the party hats she'd bought on a whim the evening before.

She put on her robe, made her coffee and watched from the bay window until the sun fully rose and the bird gave up and flew away. Her insides ached

with longing for her mother's birthday traditions—
vacation day, coffee, shopping, noodles for lunch at a
trendy fusion restaurant, more shopping, an afternoon
iced tea, then to Mom's for dinner, followed by home-
made lemon cheesecake. She dreaded the thought of
now having to create new traditions, alone.

After the bird had flown and the coffee cup had
been emptied, Whitney sighed. "Just get me through
the day, God," she said, peeling herself away from the
window. "And give Mom a hug. I'm sure she's upset
that we're apart on my birthday, too."

Her phone buzzed. It was her friend Cindy.

"Hey, girl, happy birthday! I have a song for you!"
Cindy took a deep breath. *"Haaaaaaappy bir—"*

Whitney laughed. "No! Thanks, but let's just let
you *not* singing be my birthday gift this year."

"Ouch. Harsh." Cindy giggled. "But earned."

Cindy and Whitney had become fast friends years
ago, when they started their nursing jobs at the same
hospital on the same day. Whitney had soon after
invited Cindy to church, and Cindy had taken to it
instantly. They'd been youth group coleaders ever
since. Cindy was a ray of sunshine, so funny and in-
valuable in helping Whitney get past the loss of her
mother. One of the best things about Cindy was that
she could laugh at herself; she never took it personally when people made fun of her singing. Which
was, by all accounts, truly horrible.

"Are you ready to hit that trail?" Cindy asked. "I've
had three of the kids text me already this morning.
They're pumped."

"Just about," Whitney said. "Have you talked to the others?"

"Rob is already at the church making sure the bus is good to go. But we both know he's probably just pacing and looking at his watch every five seconds. He's beyond excited about this."

"Little-kid excited?"

"Wagging-dog excited."

"Whoa," Whitney laughed. "That's excited. And what about Jeremy?"

Cindy paused. Their newest coleader had been a source of frustration for Cindy. Having only recently moved from leading the kids' group to the teens' in order to follow his daughter, he was, as Cindy once said in hushed tones, *"nothing but the word* no." The kids sometimes called him *Mr. No-No* when he wasn't around, something that Cindy and Whitney discouraged, but didn't exactly argue with. Because it was true. Jeremy watched over his daughter like a hawk and vetoed any activity that had them doing much more than sitting on the old, saggy couches in the church basement rec room. Even then, he didn't exactly look like someone who wanted to be there, and Whitney often found herself wondering why he was.

"I doubt he's too excited," Cindy finally said.

"Is he staying behind?" Whitney asked, unsure which way she wanted her friend to answer. Jeremy was vigilant, but he wasn't unkind. He was also handsome, with carefully combed brown hair, a strong jaw and pensive brown eyes. There was a tidiness to him—he looked like he chose his clothing carefully—and he left a faint trail of cologne behind him when he walked through a room. But, despite the fastidiousness, he was muscular and tan enough to suggest that he wasn't afraid to tackle the outdoors when it was called for. Sometimes when Whitney regarded Jeremy, the phrase "still waters run deep" ran through her thoughts. But there was something about him that felt more than still—there was an unmistakable hint of loneliness behind that stillness. Fellowship during a long hike might do him some real good.

"Oh, he's going," Cindy said.

"Well, I'm glad," Whitney said. "I think it will be good for Sam. She's starting to really click with some of the other kids."

"I suppose. It'll be good for her *if* he lets her have any fun."

"Well, we will just have to make sure he does," Whitney said. "We can put him in charge of another group. It'll drive him crazy, but Sam will have a great time."

"Uh-huh, and how do you know she will? What if she's afraid of her own shadow just like her dad?"

"Because, silly. It's my birthday. Everyone's going to have a great time."

This, truly, was her birthday wish. She doubted that, without her mother, she would have a *great* time, exactly. Candle Mountain would never be lemon cheesecake and fusion noodles. But maybe it would be a good distraction that could pose as a great time.

For a little while, at least.

* * *

An hour later, they were all on a bus, driving the hour-long trip to Glowing Pines Trail—the trail that led up Candle Mountain. Early fall in the Ozarks was mild, with warm glowing days and nights that were crisp rather than cold. The sun took on a golden hue, pulling back from the intensity of summer. While there was little as spectacular to look at as dogwood and redbud flowers prancing up and down the mountains in the spring, Whitney always thought the fiery colors of turning maple and white oak leaves against the green backdrop of the shortleaf pines was a sight that could nearly stop your breath. Sometimes, if you caught the seasons just right, the view across the hills of the Ozarks looked like a multicolored carpet, one that Whitney felt compelled to take off her shoes and sink her bare toes into, if only she could.

The kids were singing camp songs, led by Cindy, in the back of the bus, of course. Rob wore a gung ho smile, full of confidence and energy as he drove, and Whitney sat sideways in her seat, studying Jeremy, who was across the aisle, silently staring out the window at the passing scenery. She wondered if he, too, was imagining himself trotting across the tops of the trees. Probably not. He didn't really seem the trotting type.

He sat ramrod straight and was wearing recently pressed hiking shorts with a moisture-wicking tee. He couldn't have been more different from Rob, who wore a half-marathon T-shirt with the sleeves messily hacked off, and a pair of shorts that looked like they'd been worn and discarded onto a bedroom floor multiple times. Whitney couldn't help pondering if Jeremy was always this uptight, or if it was something about the youth group that put him on edge. Maybe he was the kind of person who needed someone else to be the conversation starter.

That was it. She needed to take the first step.

"I have cupcakes," she said.

Startled, he turned away from the window. "I'm sorry?"

She grinned, hoping her smile would be contagious. "For the party. On the peak? I brought cupcakes. Lemon." And, without knowing why she wanted to share this information with him, "It's my birthday."

"She's thirty. Old lady!" one of the kids—Stella—said from the seat behind Jeremy's. Whitney crossed her eyes at Stella and stuck out her tongue. Stella laughed uproariously. "Just kidding. About the old lady part. Not about the thirty part, though." She then went back to gabbing with the girl sharing her seat.

Whitney rolled her eyes playfully. *Teens, am I right?* But Jeremy seemed to miss the cue.

"Happy birthday," he said. A sharp laugh distracted his attention. He swiveled to find the source, then settled back into his original pose.

"Thanks!" Whitney said. "I brought candles, too. And party hats. It's going to be a real celebration."

He squinted. "How long do you plan to be up there?"

"Not long. A cupcake, a few pictures in party hats,

maybe a song. Here's a pro tip, though—cover your ears if Cindy starts singing. It's bad. She already tried to song-bomb me once today." She laughed, but he didn't join her. Jeremy was a seriously tough crowd.

"But there's a storm in the forecast."

Whitney waved the thought away. "The storm isn't supposed to get here until this evening. We've got tons of time. We'll be off the mountain before the first clouds roll in. Rob planned it out carefully. Right, Rob?"

"You betcha!" Rob yelled, never tearing his eyes away from the road. "We've even got some wiggle room."

"See? Wiggle room," she repeated, turning her palms up in a shrug, as if to say, *Who can argue with wiggle room*?

"If they're right about when the storm's going to get here," Jeremy said. "Meteorology is a tricky science. It could come early."

"If it does, we'll eat cupcakes on the bus," Whitney said, trying not to sound as deflated as she was starting to feel. She was beginning to understand Cindy's frustration. There was *careful*, and there was *Mr. No-No*. "But even if we're eating them on the bus, you still have to wear the hat. I insist."

The glimmer of a grin that finally tipped up the corners of Jeremy's mouth warmed her. He sure made a person work to get a smile, but when he did, the payoff was worth the wait. He was even more handsome when he smiled. And he was a thinker. She could practically see him mentally working out the timeline, running through all the possible scenarios. She could see him make the decision to relax… Or at least to appear relaxed.

"I'll wear it," he said. "But it may take two cupcakes to get me to agree."

"It's a deal," Whitney said, holding a hand out across the aisle. Jeremy looked at it with surprise, then reached out and shook it. Whitney sank back into her seat. "Don't think I'll forget, either, mister. You're part of the party now, whether you want to be or not."

Chapter Two

Jeremy decidedly *did not* want to be part of the party.

It wasn't anything personal. Whitney seemed like a perfectly nice person. Fun, even. She probably liked to dance and she probably told charming jokes and she probably ate the icing off of her cupcake before eating the cake. She had an open, warm face, with big green eyes and an easy smile. A sweetheart face, his mom would have called it, meaning heart shaped. There was something about Whitney that was just so natural. She probably looked forward to occasions that would necessitate a party hat. And she probably looked cute in one, with her honey-brown braids snaking out from under it.

But there was a storm coming.

In fact, as far as Jeremy was concerned, these youth group leaders were crazy for even thinking about going up that mountain, much less taking a couple dozen teenagers with them. Had they not seen the forecast? *Reckless*. That was really the only word he could think of for their decisions. And he couldn't believe he'd agreed to go with them. And to take his daughter, Sam, up with him. As an insurance risk assessor, he knew exactly what could happen and why they should have delayed the trip.

But as a dad, he wasn't surprised at all that he was sitting on this bus agreeing to *be part of the party*. Sam begged; he caved. Story of his life.

It was those dimples of hers. They reminded him so much of Laura. He'd said it the very day Sam was born—*she has your dimples*. But she didn't. Not technically. Sam had Sam's dimples, and Laura had Laura's dimples. And Laura's dimples were gone. Those dimples had been in the ground for three years now, and he would never coax them out with a corny joke again. Sam's dimples were merely a beautiful consolation. Yes, he loved to see them bloom on her cheeks nearly as much as he'd loved to see them on Laura's. But it wasn't the same. Not exactly.

Three years. That made Sam twelve, and Jeremy the most unsure single father who had ever lived. No exaggeration. The fear he'd felt when she was nine and he was all she had left was nothing compared to what he was feeling now that she was poised to embark on her journey into her teens. What if she became surly? What if—no, make that *when*—she had questions that only a mother could answer? What would he do?

He would get the job done, that's what. He would research and he would channel Laura and he would make it happen, because his job was to take care of that baby—er, young lady—the way that Laura had intended to. It was a job he took very, very seriously. And if that made him a serious man—a *not-part-of-the-party* man—he was okay with it.

Those early days after Laura's death were the hardest of his life. Trying to make a nine-year-old understand that a stranger with a gun had walked into her mother's restaurant, taken all of the money in the cash register and then, for no reason whatsoever, killed her, had seemed impossible. He could barely grasp it himself. He was never sure if he handled it right. If Sam really understood, or if all she took from his explanation was, *restaurants are where bad men are.*

They didn't visit a single restaurant for six solid months. And never went back to Laura's restaurant, period. He thought of those as their macaroni and cheese months. They ate so much boxed macaroni and cheese, they practically sweated cheese. Some days he missed those months, because the truth of it was while Sam grew older and more secure, he never did. Part of him still worried that restaurants *were* where bad men went. Men with guns, who could just walk in and destroy someone's entire world in the amount of time it took to squeeze a trigger. Restaurants and schools. And museums and skating rinks and parking lots and department stores and… So many places where a young teen would go. So many places where she could be taken from him. His own front yard.

He knew he had to fight against those fears, though. He'd been fighting them for three years, and most of the time he wasn't sure if he would call the fight successful.

These days, Sam reminded him more and more of Laura, and yet he was supposed to ease up on the reins a little. There would only be more sleepovers, more birthday parties, more school dances. He could almost hear Laura in the back of his mind, reminding him that he needed to keep their baby safe. But he could also hear her chuckling at his uncertainty. Just as she did the first few times he tried to change Sam's diaper, bathe her, give her a bottle. She'd found his inexperience charming. He'd found it frustrating. But at least then he had her to fall back on. She just seemed to know what to do. Always.

Oh, how he missed her. One of the worst things about losing the love of your life was knowing that you'd already had your Great Love and would never have it again. Why even try? Dating seemed silly and pointless. A distraction from parenting. A waste of time.

He would rather spend his time being there for Sam as much as humanly possible.

This new youth group, though. It was testing him. They were so set on adventure. Doing ridiculous things like hiking up a mountain with a storm in the forecast.

Oh, they had a plan, they said. He was willing to bet that their plan involved a whole bunch of prayer. Prayer was nice, but what did it really do to protect and save someone? Nobody was more dedicated to prayer than Laura, and look where that got her. Look where it got him and Sam. Quite frankly, he was angry about it. Prayer was a necessary part of the youth group, and he would let Sam participate because she wanted to. But he, personally, was on a hiatus from God. A permanent one, as far as he was concerned.

This reckless youth group didn't need prayer. They needed a meteorologist and common sense.

But the hike was important to Sam. She had friends going, and friends were essential, right? And they were tweens now. Too old for the kids' group. Time to move up. Time to embark on adventures. Even poorly thought out adventures.

"Your pack is pretty full there," his coleader, Whitney said, pointing at the backpack between his feet on the bus floor. For some reason, she felt compelled to talk to him throughout this entire ride. "Looks heavy. There's no way I could carry that all the way up the mountain. Mine has nothing in it compared to yours."

"I haven't done a lot of hiking," was all Jeremy had to say. "And I'm not sure today is the best day to start."

She chuckled. "We'll be off the mountain before the sun sets."

"All kinds of things can happen between now and then," he said. "Someone needs to be equipped." He realized, only when he saw her recoil, her smile fading just a bit, that he'd put a harsh emphasis on the word *someone*. He hadn't meant to offend; he was just on edge. He cleared his throat and softened his voice. He didn't like the hurt on her face. "I'm glad you're carrying the cupcakes, though. Those wouldn't make it all the way up the mountain if I were carrying them."

Her smile reappeared and something in him lightened. "They'll taste better at the peak. I'm sure of it. I can't wait to get up there and find out," she said.

"Wow, you're really nothing but excited about this, aren't you?"

She shrugged. "Well, it *is* my birthday. I'll get to celebrate with sugar while looking out over the world. What's not to be excited about?"

He gave her an encouraging nod, and tried to feel encouraged himself, but it wasn't working. He was sinking back into his thoughts—going over preparedness rules in his head—when she reached over and touched his shoulder, pulling him into the present. "Don't worry," she said. "It's going to be fun. Rob is a super hiker. He does this all the time. Right, Rob?"

"Yup," Rob said from the driver's seat. "This is my tenth trek up the Candle."

"See? He's experienced. If he says it's safe, it's safe. Trust him."

Trust. Now that was an interesting concept. What had Jeremy trusted since Laura was killed? Nothing. How did you trust a world that turned on you like the flip of a switch?

Instinctively, his gaze shifted to find Sam, who was sitting several rows behind him. She was braiding some colorful string with the girl next to her, laughing and being silly and just so… Happy. He smiled in spite of himself.

His daughter was beautiful. Her joy was beautiful. That was one thing he could trust.

The bus took a wide right turn and a couple of the kids—the ones who weren't dramatically holding on as if they were on a roller coaster—took to their windows.

"We're here," he heard Sam say, her voice laced with awe and excitement. She briefly glanced up and his eyes met hers. She gave a double fist pump of excitement and put on the pink, glittery sunglasses she'd made him buy for the trip. She clowned, posing like a movie star wearing her new shades. He could tell she was trying to quell his worries. Sam was sensitive like that. She knew when he was wary. She didn't usually fight it—just let him do what he felt he needed to do to protect her. But sometimes, very rarely, she let him know that she thought he was *being too much*. Her words. Seemed like the moment she turned twelve, those times began happening more frequently. And then he was the one doing the quelling.

He gave her a thumbs-up with a smile meant to say, *Yes, this is exciting, all good*, then craned to see out the windshield as Rob eased the bus into a parking space. The lot was full. Hikers were tumbling out of their cars and trucks and buses in various states of preparedness, from those wearing tennis shoes and cutoff jeans and carrying nothing other than car keys and a water bottle, to those toting bulging backpacks with attached tent rolls.

He suddenly felt silly for how full his pack was. Maybe Whitney was right, and he was overprepared.

Maybe his overpreparedness would embarrass Sam, and later, when they got home, she would chastise him for *being too much*, and she would be angry and he would feel like he let not only Sam down, but in some weird way, he'd let Laura down, too.

Don't be such a risk assessor, Laura used to say when he would go into *what-if* mode. He could practically feel her pat his cheek the way she used to do when she found him to be unreasonable and unreasonably cute at the same time. Involuntarily, his hand floated to his cheek. These were the thoughts he wrestled with daily, it seemed. Balance. He couldn't find it. He wasn't even sure he was capable of it anymore. He only knew that he had to keep trying, for Sam.

He took a breath and reasoned through as best he could. They weren't going on an overnight, just a half day. He likely wouldn't need all the food he'd packed. He didn't need two full first aid kits—one would suffice. Water filter, freeze-dried fruit, flashlights. Those were things that were in the overnighters' packs. The ones who would take the meandering western trail up Glowing Pine Mountain to Pine Peak, the looming neighboring mountain pushed up against the Candle and took two days to traverse.

He glanced at the pack, back to Sam and then to Whitney, who had shouldered her own, much lighter, bag. Whitney was smiling back at him, looking almost as eager about the hike as Sam did. As if she needed her own glittery pink sunglasses.

Rob popped open the bus door, and the volume ratcheted up with the kids' anticipation. It always amazed him how loud just a few excited teens could get. Jeremy could barely hear himself think, and right now, he really, really needed to think.

Rob stood, turned and held both arms in the air. "Hey! Hey!" The kids settled some. "Let's keep it down to a dull roar, okay? You gotta be aware of your surroundings out here. This isn't an amusement park rendition of nature. It's *actual* nature. This trail is pretty safe, but there are some rocky patches that can get slick. You start sliding and it can be impossible to stop. Stay on the trail. The forest is dense. It can be very easy to get turned around in there. Remember all the training videos we watched over the summer?" There was a collective affirming mumble. Rob nodded. "Good. Let's try to remember what we learned while we're out here, okay?

"Now, you have your buddies already assigned. Stick with your buddy. I'll be taking the lead, since I know the trail. Miss Cindy and Mister Jeremy will be in line with y'all. If you have a problem, say something. Miss Whitney will be at the back of the line. She'll have the other one of these." He pulled a walkie-talkie off of his belt. "Again, if you have a problem, say something. We all want to come home safe, right?"

The "right" coming from the back of the bus was so loud Jeremy actually winced a little. But it seemed to thrill Rob.

"And what are you supposed to do if you have a problem?" he asked, cupping his ear.

"Say something!" the kids cried.

"Good," he said. "And don't fall off any cliffs." Now the murmur turned alarmed, and he laughed and patted the air. "Just kidding, just kidding. Let's offer up a quick prayer." The kids quieted, and Jeremy watched as they bowed their heads, some of them snickering as they poked at each other. "Lord, let us have fun, be safe and appreciate your glory in the nature that surrounds us. Amen."

A scattered chorus of *Amens* rang throughout the bus.

He didn't even mention the storm. Jeremy frowned at the thought, nonplussed.

"One more thing," Rob said. "If you don't need it, don't take it. That hill gets pretty steep, and you'll regret every stuffed animal and iPad you've got in your pack. I'm locking the bus—it's not going anywhere. Take out what you don't need and leave it here."

"Better here than the side of the trail," Cindy added. "Because we will not carry it for you if you poop out halfway up."

There was a collective sound of zipping and unzipping, and Jeremy watched as kids shed jackets, stuffed animals and handheld video games into their seats.

"Let's move out!" Rob grabbed his backpack and jumped off the bus. Whitney and Jeremy turned to face each other. She gestured for him to follow.

Don't be such a risk assessor.

"You go ahead," he said. "I need to do some adjusting."

He bent over his pack, and as Whitney and the kids filed out of the bus, he unloaded all the extraneous items, until his pack was much, much lighter.

Chapter Three

The longer they walked, the more energy the kids had. Or maybe it was the less energy Whitney had. She wasn't sure. It seemed like only yesterday that she would've been goofing off with her friends on a long hike—bounding ahead, jogging backward, stopping to laugh and then skipping to catch up again. She wouldn't have even noticed being out of breath or feeling like her calves were on fire.

She noticed those things now. But she didn't mind. A good hike was a good workout, and besides, there was so much to look at, and the kids were missing it all.

The trail went from paved by the parking lot to packed dirt to rocky and rutted, with twisting tree roots searching for new ground. The forest had gotten so dense, at times the trail felt more like a tunnel, which was a respite from the sun. In the shade, the depths of the woods were darker, more mysterious, like something out of a fairy tale. Squirrels darted about, curious and hungry. A startled rabbit rushed out of the bushes on one side of the trail and in two leaps had disappeared into the bushes on the other side. Whitney gasped and stumble-stepped, her heart catching, and then laughed at her own jumpiness. The kids were oblivious to it all.

The walkie-talkie squawked to life, a bunch of static with a muddled voice threaded through it. She pulled it out of her waistband and pressed the button on the side. "Come again?" she asked.

More static, more distorted vocal sounds, no actual words.

"I can't understand you. You're all garbled up."

She'd inadvertently slowed, and the kids had rounded a corner without her. Now she had to hurry to catch up. She felt a bead of sweat roll between her shoulder blades. It was the climbing making her perspire. She knew the air would be chilly at the peak, drying up the sweat, and by the time they got back to the bus, evening would be settling on them and she'd be ready for her jacket, which she kept tied around her waist.

Finally, she saw the backs of Stella, Annie and Lucy—the three dawdlers—as they ambled along. They'd been picking up leaves and were twisting them into a rope that dragged behind them.

"Girls!" she shouted. They turned around. She shook the walkie-talkie above her head. "Find out what Mister Rob wanted."

They'd been doing this all morning. The walkies had been a great idea, if only they'd worked well.

They'd seemed to be fine when they tested them at the church, but Whitney guessed they hadn't stood far enough apart to see how they would do on the mountain. She felt cut off from the rest of the adults. And of course, cell phone reception was all but nonexistent on this mountain, something Rob had warned them about ahead of time.

Stella shouted up the line, and Whitney heard as, kid by kid, the question got passed forward, and a wave of shouts grew louder as the answer came back toward her. Finally, Stella turned so that she was walking backward.

She cupped her hands around her mouth. "He said we are a few minutes away from the rest area!"

She had to admit, a rest sounded like the best idea ever. She hadn't drunk enough to need the bathroom—which, she would be the first to admit, was not ideal hiking behavior—but she could use the chance to catch her breath, rest her legs and reconvene with the adults.

Is this what thirty is going to be like? she wondered. *Always looking forward to your next rest stop?* She could almost hear her mother laughing, answering her: *Pshaw, you think this is bad? Wait until you hit fifty...*

Her mother couldn't have passed on any wisdom about sixty, though. She never got there—a fact that Whitney was painfully aware of, it seemed, every second of the day. It wasn't just that Whitney was a mama's girl—it was that she was a mama's best friend. Her dad had died in a car accident when she was fifteen, so for just shy of half of her life, her mom was literally all she had. They'd weathered every storm together and had done it with the kind of bravery that only comes with knowing you have one cohort in this world. Someone who is going through it—whatever it is—with you.

Whitney had no more had that thought than she heard a noise just off-trail in the woods. The same *knock-knock-knock* she'd awakened to that morning. She stopped dead in her tracks, her shoes skidding in the loose rock. She lifted her hand to shade her eyes from the sun and spun in place until she found it, about thirty feet into the woods, clinging to a rotting tree.

Black-and-white. Red tuft on top.

"What in the world?" she said aloud.

She had literally never seen a woodpecker in her life, and now this was twice in one day. She watched as it banged on the tree, her mind swirling with the insane thought that it could be the same one that was at her house that morning. Even though she knew that was highly unlikely and kind of ridiculous, she couldn't help herself. The whole thing was kind of ridiculous. Waking up to a woodpecker knocking on your door was ridiculous.

Voices floated along the trail—kids reenergizing as they neared the rest stop. Whitney knew she needed to catch up, but she was rooted right where she was. She couldn't help it.

"Mom?" She whispered, feeling silly, while at the same time, totally reasonable. "Is that you?"

A couple appeared behind her, breaking the spell. They looked very touristy, with button-down Hawaiian shirts, visors shading their eyes from the sun and pristine hiking boots. The woman held a camera, and the man had a pair of binoculars looped around his neck.

"Excuse me," the woman said. "Do you know if there's a rest area on this trail? We heard there was, but it seems like we should have run across it by now."

"Oh," Whitney said. "Yes, it's just ahead. If you look through there you can kind of see it." She pointed into the trees, through which she could just barely see patches of brick and movement of bodies. "It's right around the next bend."

"Thank you," the woman said.

"Spot something interesting?" the man asked, picking up the binoculars.

Whitney laughed. "A woodpecker." She pointed toward the tree. "It's the weirdest thing. One woke me up this morning knocking on my door, and here's anoth—"

The woodpecker was gone.

Had it been a figment of her imagination? Surely not. She'd heard *and* seen him. Twice. In one day. She spun again, searching.

"He's not there anymore," she said sheepishly. "He was pretty, though."

"Downy, redheaded, red-bellied or pileated?" the man asked. He rotated his torso while scanning the woods with the binoculars.

"Oh, gosh, I wouldn't know," Whitney said. "I don't really know anything about birds."

"Did its call sound like a trill or a chortle or a squawk?"

"I didn't… I only heard knocking," Whitney said.

The woman put her hand on the man's arm. "Barry here's a birder. We've seen so many interesting species on this trail. He loves woodpeckers. We haven't seen one yet today, have we, Barry?"

"Unfortunately, no." Barry lowered his binoculars. "They say if you see a woodpecker, you need to pay attention," he said sagely.

"Why?"

He shrugged. "It's just a superstition, of course. You know, opportunity is knocking, and all that."

"Oh." Whitney smiled. "Well, maybe it means I'm about to get rich."

"Or maybe it's all a bunch of hooey," the woman said. "Like I said, Barry knows everything there is to know about birds. Even some things that are a little more on the fictional side."

Barry peered through his binoculars again, paying no attention to the woman's critique. He let them drop against his chest. "I've never seen a red-bellied," he said. "Sure would've made my day. We're not from around here. We don't get them on the West Coast."

"Sorry," Whitney said. "Would have made mine, too, if it had still been there."

"Well," the woman said. "It would make my day to get to that rest stop. I don't know about you, but I'm tired."

Whitney nodded and smiled but allowed them to go on while she continued to scour the trees for the woodpecker.

"Opportunity is knocking, huh?" she whispered. "Weird."

When her walkie squawked again, she jumped back into motion, following the trail onto what looked like a gravel parking lot, only lined with benches instead of parking spaces. A squat, square restroom was tucked off to one side, pushed so far up against the trees it was almost in them. A line had formed at the door of the women's side. Scattered around the perimeter of the clearing were hikers, staring out at the spectacular view, studying the distance and taking photos. Whitney marveled at the elevation they'd climbed already. No wonder she'd been so winded. Yet the mountain only got steeper from here.

She headed to an empty bench and unloaded her pack, unwound her jacket and stuffed it inside, then took a moment to enjoy the rolling forest view. Cindy sidled up to her, wiping wet hands on the back of her shorts.

"Gorgeous, isn't it?" Cindy asked.

"It really is. Although *that's* not my favorite view," Whitney answered, gesturing toward the line outside the ladies' room. It had shrunk as some of the youth group girls spilled out and started taking selfies, but it was still long.

"Only three stalls," Cindy said. "And Lily has one of the stalls tied up." She held her stomach and puffed her cheeks out as if she were going to be sick. Lily was one of their younger teens. She'd looked perfectly fine on the bus that morning.

"Oh, no," Whitney said. "Is it the altitude?"

Cindy shrugged. "Maybe a bug that hit at a really bad time? We're two hours away from the bus, and two hours away from the peak. And the climbing gets more intense from here. She barely made it here. She'll have to stop and chuck every three steps. We're going to have to figure something out. Oh, there's Rob and Jeremy!" She stood on her tiptoes and waved them over.

"I'll join you in a minute," Whitney said, "Watch my pack?"

"Sure thing," Cindy said. "Hey, Rob, we've got a situation…"

Whitney took her time in the restroom and happened to be at the sink when Lily finally emerged from the stall. She was pale and waxy, her hair stuck to her neck with sweat.

"Oh, honey, you don't look so good," Whitney said.

"I don't feel so good," Lily affirmed. She tried to spool out a paper towel, but the dispenser was empty. "I think I need to go back."

Whitney grimaced. "Are you sure?" She removed the folded bandanna Lily had been using for a headband and wet it under the cold tap.

"I'm all shaky," Lily said. "I can't walk uphill anymore. I want my mom."

Whitney squeezed excess water out of the bandanna and pressed it against the back of Lily's neck.

Lily placed her hands on either side of the sink and leaned forward, taking deep breaths in through her nose and out through her mouth. Whitney could see goose bumps on the girl's arms.

"I'm sure we can figure something out. Miss Cindy's talking to the other leaders about it right now." Whitney handed the cloth back to Lily, rubbed her back a little, gave her an encouraging smile and guided her out of the restroom.

All of the youth group kids had congregated into a large—loud—circle. Rob, Cindy and Jeremy still stood together nearby. Whitney deposited Lily on the bench where she'd left her backpack; Lily immediately pulled her knees up and rested her forehead on them.

"…guess that's the only choice, then," Rob said. He checked his watch. "But Jeremy's right, we're going to run out of time if we don't get moving. So I say we just go with that."

"With what?" Whitney asked.

"I'm going to take Lily back down to the bus," Cindy said. "Try to get her parents to pick her up. And then I'll either meet you here on your way back down, or just wait for you at the bus, depending on when they get here. Good thing there are four of us, huh? Jeremy, you're okay taking the middle by yourself?"

Jeremy cleared his throat and nodded solemnly, as if he'd just been assigned a very important mission. "Yeah, not a problem," he said.

"Okay, chickie, let's go," Cindy said, holding out a hand to Lily.

The teen looked up from her lap, smiled weakly and took Cindy's hand. "I'm sorry," she croaked. She stood and shouldered her backpack.

Cindy waved it away. "Girl, there's nothing to be sorry about. I didn't really want to go all the way to the peak anyway. I've got my cardio for the day. And I've been up there before. It's not that big of a deal. Just a bunch of rocks and the tops of a lot of trees." She patted Whitney's shoulder as they walked by. "Save me a cupcake, okay?"

"Sure thing."

"All right," Rob called to the kids. "Everyone have their partners? Good! Let's get moving again. We'll need to pick up the pace a little. We've lost some time." He gave Whitney and Jeremy a thumbs-up and jogged back to the trail. The kids followed him in excited little clusters, some of them eating the snacks they'd pulled out of their packs. He slowed to a fast walk but didn't stop. Whitney could tell he was determined to make up time.

Jeremy hurried to catch up, submerging himself in the thick of the group.

Whitney sighed. She was disappointed that she wouldn't get to celebrate her birthday with Cindy. But she supposed they could eat a quick cupcake in the church parking lot afterward. Whitney would tell Cindy about the peak party and how it was just not the same without her. Maybe she would even tell her about the woodpecker.

She looked around, scanning the trees and the restroom roof, searching for the telltale red crown, but saw none. Once again, she glanced at the sky, silently giving her mom a knowing side-eye. She knew it was preposterous to think that just because she saw a bird in the woods, it meant her mother was somehow following her. But she couldn't help it—losing someone important to you really did a number on your thoughts.

By the time she turned her attention back to the present, the group was completely gone, having disappeared around a bend. With a jolt, she reached for her pack, but before she could get the straps over her shoulders, Jeremy came jogging back down the trail toward her. Probably worried that she wasn't with them.

She waved. "Sorry! I'm coming! I got sidetr—"

He hadn't slowed, and now that he was in view, she could see that something was wrong. She dropped her pack and hurried to close the gap between them.

"What's going on?"

"Sam," was all he said, as he veered around her, heading straight for the restroom, his pack bouncing on his back. He pounded on the ladies' room door. "Sam?"

Whitney caught up with him. "Is she sick, too?"

He shrugged. "I have no idea. She was Lily's partner, so nobody noticed she was missing. I figured it out when I did a head count. She's not on the trail."

"Okay," Whitney said. "I'll go in and check on her."

She pushed past the line, went inside the restroom and called out. "Sam? You in here? Everything okay, sweetie?" She bent to check under stall doors. She didn't know what kind of shoes Sam was wearing, so she called again. "Sam? Your dad's worried."

No response. She felt a blast of adrenaline that turned her cold.

"Sam?"

There was a flush, and a woman came out of one of the stalls. Whitney stepped back to let the woman get past her, then started knocking on the other stall doors.

"Sam, you need to say something *now* if you're in here."

But there was still no response. Sam was not in the restroom.

Whitney bolted back outside where Jeremy waited with the most painfully expectant look on his face. She shook her head.

"You're absolutely sure she wasn't in the group?" she asked.

"Yes, I'm absolutely sure," he said, his voice edged with irritation that Whitney tried not to take personally. She didn't have a daughter, but she imagined that if she did, she would be going crazy right now. "I walked the entire line, counting them off. We should have had an odd number, and we didn't. She's not there. I can't believe nobody noticed that she wasn't with us. All that nonsense about sticking together…"

"Maybe she went around to the other side of the building?" Whitney asked, although she couldn't imagine why. She scrambled around the perimeter of the entire building, and even stopped and gazed into the woods, but saw no sign of Sam.

"Sam?" Jeremy was still calling into the restroom when Whitney came back.

Whitney's heart was really pounding now. Cindy had no walkie, so Whitney couldn't radio to make sure Sam hadn't followed her partner down the mountain. But she couldn't imagine Cindy letting Sam do that without communicating with someone somehow. She would have dragged Lily back up the mountain if she'd had to. She would've known they'd be worried sick.

She locked eyes with Jeremy, and he seemed to understand exactly what she wasn't saying.

Something was wrong. Very wrong.

Jeremy took off around the building, as if to verify what Whitney hadn't found.

Whitney pulled the walkie out of her waistband and pressed the button on the side. "Rob?" she said. "Can you hear me?"

There was a cut-up, nonsensical response, barely more than static. She pushed the button again, thankful that he was still close enough for the radio to reach.

"We have a problem. Come back to the rest stop. I think one of our kids is lost."

Chapter Four

Rob had not immediately replied, but Whitney tucked her walkie back in her waistband anyway. Her mind was racing with what Sam's disappearance could mean. Part of her wanted to reassure herself that it meant nothing. Sam was a smart girl who knew how to watch out for herself. She would make a fuss if someone tried to take her. Besides, anyone wanting to kidnap a kid wouldn't wait until a busy rest stop to do it, especially not with two hours on either side of them for an escape.

Sam was also smart enough not to go off-trail. Why would she? Her friends were on the trail. Her partner was on the trail. The restroom was on the trail. Her dad—*her* dad, of all people!—was on the trail, watching her like a hawk. They'd been warned and watched videos, and Sam had good common sense.

No, she hadn't been kidnapped, and she wasn't lost in the forest. There must have been another, more logical explanation for what happened to her. But Whitney couldn't find it. It was as if the child had disappeared into thin air.

Maybe Jeremy overlooked her in the throng of kids. Maybe somehow she was in the restroom and Whitney missed it. Maybe she really had gone with Cindy, and Cindy didn't have a chance yet to get her back up to the rest stop.

But there was that small possibility.

Whitney shaded her eyes and peered into the woods. She tried to remember what Sam was wearing but couldn't.

Jeremy had circled the building again, and now she could see him coming toward her.

"Nothing?" he asked.

Whitney shook her head. "I'm sure there's no reason to panic, though," she said. "We just have to think. We know she's not in the restroom, and we know she's not behind the building. I'm certain Cindy wouldn't have kept her, and you're certain that she wasn't with the group. She wouldn't have gone off with a stranger, would she?"

"No. No way," Jeremy said, although he noticeably blanched at the thought of it.

"I don't think she would, either," Whitney said. "I'm sure she wouldn't."

"So she went into the woods." His voice sounded tight. "It's the only possible explanation."

Whitney wanted to argue. Surely it wasn't the only possible explanation. She hated dealing in absolutes. As a nurse, she'd learned that sometimes things hap-

pened that absolutes couldn't explain. People woke up
from comas, people died thirty seconds after laughing at a joke or thirty days after learning they had
a condition. People responded to medications that
shouldn't work and didn't respond to medications that
should. Her supervisor explained it best one horrible
night when a woman lost her baby three weeks before
she was due: life is chaos. Science explained what it
could, but good science knew when to get out of the
way. That's when faith stepped in to help navigate
through the turmoil.

Life is chaos. Sam's disappearance may or may not
have fallen under that theory. Whitney sure hoped
she hadn't gone into the woods, but she couldn't ignore the possibility.

"I can't remember what she was wearing." Too
late, Whitney realized they should've had colorful
youth group T-shirts made for easy spotting.

"Red," he said. "I told her she needed to wear
something bright just in case she…" He trailed off,
peering hard into the woods, and Whitney could see
tension straining his neck and shoulders. "Although
now that I think about it, I'm pretty sure she took
the red jacket off on the bus. I don't know if she put
it back on."

"Okay, so we wait here until we can figure out
where she might have gone," Whitney said. "I've radi-
oed Rob. I'm sure they're headed back this direction."

"But if they're not?"

"I'm sure they are," she repeated. "And I'm sure
there are park rangers around. If she's out there,

they'll find her. She's twelve. How far can she really go?"

He glanced from the woods to Whitney and back again. It was more than tension that he wore. It was terror. And it seemed like the more she talked, the worse it got. A twelve-year-old could go plenty far.

"We can't just stay here and decide what to do later," he said. "My daughter is missing. I'm not going to sit back and wait for an answer to come to me."

"Okay, let's call 9-1-1." She instinctively reached for her phone but was disappointed to see that it still wasn't picking up any service. "Is your phone working?"

His hand slipped to his pocket. He pulled a phone out, held it up. "No. I don't have any bars—" His head jutted forward and he squinted into the trees. "Wait. Is that…?" He dashed off into the woods about twenty feet, bent and picked up something. Whitney couldn't believe he'd even seen it. She still couldn't see what it was, even though it was in his hand.

She followed him, taking care not to trip over brush or slip on a loose rock or turn her ankle in a rut. When she got to him, she could see that he was holding a pair of sunglasses with pink, glittery frames.

"She was here," he said.

"You don't know that for sure," Whitney argued. "These could have come from anyone." Although when she thought about it, she could remember Sam wearing something very similar as she got off the bus. The likelihood that those had belonged to someone else was very low.

He shook his head. "No. She insisted that I buy these for the hike. Something has happened. There are cliffs out here. And wild animals."

Whitney's brain raced with ideas, trying to remember all the things they'd learned about mountaineering safety. What to do if someone got separated from the group was a big one. But the words *cliffs* and *wild animals* had rattled her, and her thoughts were swirling too fast to remember any of what was said. She'd never considered how urgent it would feel if it was discovered that someone could be lost.

"Okay, let's be calm," she said, but she knew that her voice wasn't calm. She also knew that it was a waste of her time to try to calm him. Sam was his daughter. It didn't take an expert to know that on the inside he was panicking. Whitney tried to use the technique she'd used as a young ER nurse. Whenever she'd get rattled, she would take ten seconds to mentally list all of the things she could see and hear around her. The list would root her into reality and take her out of *what-if* mode, and it actually worked.

"I'm going to find her," Jeremy said before she could even list one thing. Before Whitney could argue, he plunged deeper into the woods.

Torn, Whitney glanced at the back of the restroom, which already had the appearance of being a million miles away, and as if it was—or they were—being swallowed by the woods. Going farther into the forest was a definite no-no in mountaineering safety, of that she was sure. But she was also sure that if Sam was out there, it probably wasn't ideal for Jeremy to be out there alone looking for her.

With one last bit of hesitation, Whitney followed him.

They were off-trail, and like Rob warned, it didn't take long for the terrain to be rough. Weeds grasped at their ankles and shins as they climbed up and up, trying to get to a place where they could see more than a few feet in front of them. They were moving quickly. Too quickly to keep from getting too far away from the trail, Whitney thought. The longer they walked, the less likely it seemed to her that Sam would've gone this far in. But they were moving at too fast a clip for her to say anything.

"Sam?" Jeremy hollered. "Sam!" Nothing in return but birdsong and the crunch of their shoes on dead leaves.

Whitney finally got close enough to grasp a portion of his sleeve. "I think we're going the wrong way. She wouldn't have gone this far, would she?"

"If she got confused, she could have."

"I think we should reevaluate. Come up with a plan," Whitney said. She gazed around herself. She felt closed in by the forest. She had a good idea which direction the rest area was, but she could no longer see it—a totally disconcerting feeling.

He was right. It wouldn't take long to get confused and go the wrong direction, and she could definitely see a panicked twelve-year-old accidentally getting lost and being too upset to stop moving and wait for someone to come to her. "We have a better chance of finding her if we have a plan. We keep going up the mountain, but what if she went down?"

"You're right," Jeremy finally said. She could feel his intensity, his desire to keep going. "You backtrack. Go down that way. I'll keep going this way. We'll cover both."

Another mountaineering safety nugget popped into her head—*do not split up.* They'd pounded the partner rule into the kids' heads from day one. *Stay together, stay together, stay together.* But she also heard the slight quaver in his voice. He was scared for his daughter. Besides, if Whitney was alone, she could walk more slowly, search more deliberately, instead of just trying to keep up. She could get on the walkie-talkie and let Rob know what they were doing.

"Okay," she said. She pivoted and began going back the direction they'd come, ducking under branches and looking for clear spaces for her feet. Going down the mountain was somehow scarier than going up. It was as if gravity were working with the vegetation to tug her faster and faster.

"Sam!" she heard Jeremy call, coming from what already sounded far away. She knew he was nearby—they'd only just separated—how was it so easy to get swallowed by these woods? The very thought terrified her. If it was this easy for two adults, she could imagine how easy it would be for a relatively small twelve-year-old.

She made sure her calls for Sam were in the lulls between Jeremy's calls. That way he knew where she was. It felt like a tether between the two of them.

After several feet, she saw a clearing, what looked like maybe an old trail. It veered away from the rest area a bit, but she thought it might provide her a view of a larger area of the woods, so she rushed toward it. She was aware that she was moving faster and with less surety than she would've liked, but urgency was starting to set in again. The quicker they could get to Sam, the sooner they could get out of these woods.

"Sam, honey? Call out for us!" she yelled, as her feet began to crunch against loose mountain rock. "Sam?"

She spun in circles, desperately looking for the girl. She saw movement and recognized the yellow of Jeremy's shirt. She wished she'd had the forethought to wear bright clothing, as well. Her gray T-shirt was light and loose fitting and had seemed like a good idea at the time. But gray didn't stick out, and she wondered if Jeremy could even see her from where he was.

She spotted a good vantage point that looked out over the tops of trees on one of the smaller hills and decided to keep moving. It seemed unlikely Sam would be all the way down there, but then again, Whitney wasn't exactly sure how far up they'd climbed before splitting.

As she walked, the area of loose rock got bigger and repeatedly rolled away from beneath her tread. She held her arms out to her sides to keep her balance, but as the grade got steeper, she found it harder to do. Gravity started to take over, and she tried to compensate by shifting her weight backward. Which was a big mistake.

She was already off balance when she hit a patch of rock that completely gave way. Her arms pinwheeled and her feet scrabbled against the ground, but that only resulted in churning up more gravel. She threw her body sideways, trying to flatten herself to the ground. There was no stopping now. In a blur, the stones carried her down and down, and she somersaulted over sharpness and grit until she stopped abruptly against the trunk of a tree. Her right foot took the brunt of the impact. She felt her ankle turn beneath her, heard a muffled pop and felt fingers of pain grasp her ankle hard.

Dizzy, she moaned, trying to clear her vision, which had gotten swimmy with the fall. Her hand went up to her head, but somehow—surprisingly—came away dry. No blood there. Her elbows were both scraped, though, and blood seeped from a gash in her knee.

But as her awareness cleared, the pain in her ankle brightened. Shock gave way to a thudding ache. She tried to get up, but when she put weight on that leg, the pain radiated upward. She cried out and fell down again.

Okay, Whitney, she thought. *You know what to do. Don't panic. Just go over your training. You've dealt with hundreds of injured ankles.*

But she hadn't dealt with them at the bottom of a cliff in the middle of the Ozark Mountains. All alone.

She rubbed her ankle and scanned the area. She'd

fallen about twenty feet down a steep grade. The cliff above, the promising vantage point where she had been headed only moments before, might as well be as far away as the moon. No way could she get back up there on this ankle. And she knew Jeremy was even higher up than that. What was more, she was no longer sure exactly which direction the rest area was. Had her fall changed it? Had she tumbled right past it? If so, she would now be looking for a trail rather than a building. From where she sat, that seemed impossible.

But she needed to get help—that was a given. She needed help for Sam, and now she needed help for herself, too. Jeremy might be too panicked to worry about getting a ranger involved, but she was not. She would call. She needed to call. *Please, God, wherever I am, let the walkie-talkie work out here.*

She reached for her waistband, but the walkie was no longer clipped to it. Feeling a jolt of alarm, she flipped to her hands and knees and felt around in the brush but couldn't find it anywhere.

Gone. This was bad, bad, bad.

Plopping down on her backside again, just about to give up, she spotted it lodged between two rocks about ten feet above her. It must have fallen off her belt on her way down.

She tried again to get up. The pain was sharp, but not unbearable. After limping a few steps, only to slide back down again, she knew that her stability was not going to get her to that walkie. She was going to have to call out for help.

Chapter Five

When Jeremy first heard the cries for help, his heart jumped to jackhammer-level pounding. He thought it was Sam calling for him. He stilled, cocking his head toward the sound, every muscle tensed to pounce in her direction.

But when he heard it again, he realized it was a woman's voice. Whitney. Immediately, his mind went to dark places—*something is wrong with Sam*. But then he remembered how Laura used to scold him for always going to the worst possible scenario in his mind.

It's a hazard of the trade, he used to say. *The better I am at seeing what could go wrong, the better I am at my job.*

But you're not at work right now, she'd say. *Sometimes things go right.*

He forced himself to consider that maybe this was one of those times. Maybe Whitney was calling out because she'd found Sam safe and sound.

"I hear you!" he shouted. "I'm coming!"

He took off toward where he thought the voice had been coming from, though every time he heard it, it seemed to be far away. Farther than it should have been. How had the distance between them grown so quickly?

He raced through brambles, tripping on the occasional root, his shoelaces getting caught by weeds. Then he would hit a rock patch and be reminded that he was actually running downhill. A few times, he slid and was nearly unable to keep his balance. He tried not to think about Sam out here in this impossible terrain, and all of the horrible things that could go wrong.

Sometimes things go right. Sometimes things go right. Sometimes...

Whitney had stopped calling out, and he paused, panting, images of every worst-case scenario pushing Laura's naive positivity right out of his head. Maybe she was now unable to call out because she was too busy resuscitating Sam, or because she didn't want to alarm the bobcat that was looming over them, or because she was bent with grief over having found his daughter's crumpled and broken body.

The way he'd been bent with grief when he'd gotten that phone call from the police three years ago. *Mr. Moon, we need you to come down to The Happy Egg, sir. It's about your wife...*

"Whitney?" he called, willing himself to come back to the present. He listened.

After a pause, "Jeremy? I'm here!"

Only it didn't make sense, because the voice seemed to come from somewhere far below him.

"Keep calling!" he yelled.

Slowly, he crept toward a cliff edge, trying not to make too much noise with his boots for fear of drowning out her calls, all the while thinking angry thoughts. *What a party, huh?* he wanted to ask. *Aren't you glad you brought cupcakes for this?* To say those things would be cruel, but it didn't stop him from thinking them. Not even Jeremy Moon, professional risk assessor, could be rational all the time.

He could almost hear Laura laugh at that thought the most, and it made him think the cruelest thought of all: *Go ahead and laugh it up. You're not the one down here raising her alone.*

"Jeremy?" Whitney called again. She sounded closer. But he still couldn't see her. Unless…

He edged forward, his every step sending cascades of rocks spilling below. He could see them roll, roll and then disappear over the drop-off. He eased forward until he could peer over the edge.

Whitney was about twenty feet down. She was pretty banged up and was sitting with her back against a tree. He could see relief wash over her when she saw his face.

"I fell," she said. The simplicity of her statement and sorrow on her face made him regret all the things he'd been thinking moments before.

"I thought you may have found Sam," he said. "Are you hurt?"

She grimaced and rubbed her ankle. "I think so. I

might be able to walk on it. But I dropped the walkie, and I can't get up there." She pointed to where the radio was nestled in the rocks.

He assessed the cliff. There was a clear path of loose rock that led right over the edge; Whitney must have happened upon the wrong spot and been taken down like a landslide.

Farther to the west, there was more vegetation. He could work his way down to her using tree roots and larger rocks for footing.

"Hang tight," he said. "I'm coming down."

He found a good spot, turned around so he was nearly on his belly and eased down using hands and feet. He was aware of Whitney murmuring encouraging words as he worked, but he couldn't make them out. He was too focused on getting to stable land without incident. The last thing they needed was for both of them to be injured. It was bad enough they were now going to have no choice but to suspend their search while they got Whitney back to the rest area for help. If he became injured, they would have to rely on others to find her. Organizing that could take way too long.

He felt a fleeting moment of bitterness at Whitney's injury, but quickly squashed it. It was unfair of him to think that way. She'd followed him into the woods out of concern for Sam. She hadn't meant to get hurt. Of that, he was sure.

He edged over to the walkie, nearly losing his footing when a large rock gave way. But somehow he hung on and got to the small radio. He was surprised to see the plastic didn't appear to be too banged up. A part of him had expected it to be shattered. With the radio secured to his waistband, he let himself slide gently the rest of the way down the cliff and made his way to her, wiping grit off of his hands.

He handed the walkie to Whitney. She fiddled with the buttons; it was still working. She tried Rob several times, but couldn't get any response. Not even static. Which, Jeremy feared, might have meant he was out of range. How far into the forest had they gone? He thought he had a general idea of where the rest area was, but he couldn't see it, and he also knew he'd been so focused on finding Sam that he hadn't paid as close attention to his whereabouts as he should have.

Regardless, he had to get Whitney back to the rest area. He filled with dread at what that could mean for Sam, especially if she was still moving… Or worse, if she, too, was injured. He didn't want this delay. He wanted to keep looking for his little girl until he had her safely in his arms. But Whitney had followed him into the woods without reservation. He couldn't let her down. It wouldn't be the right thing to do. He had to be there for her just like she was there for him.

He surveyed the area. The terrain going back where they'd come from was steep. He doubted she could traverse it on that ankle. But there was no way he could carry her through these brambles on this incline—it was precarious enough to do it alone. She was going to have to at least try to hobble up, even if it meant they moved farther away from the rest area to get to flatter ground.

"Can you put any weight on that ankle?" he asked. "We need to get you back."

"I think so. I can try," Whitney said. "Did you find any more sign of Sam?"

He shook his head.

"Maybe that's good news. Maybe it means she's not out here, and when we get back to the trail, she'll be there," Whitney said, but he could tell by the way her smile struggled to stay on that she wasn't so sure of that.

Whitney placed her hand on the tree behind her for stability, then carefully raised herself to full height. She couldn't put her all of her weight on her ankle, but she could get around. Every time she took a step, she grimaced. He reached out for her, but she waved him away.

"I'll go by myself," she said. "You can keep looking for Sam. Finding her is the most important thing."

He was taken aback with the selflessness of her offer. But even with her conviction about going it alone, he couldn't let her wander off into the woods by herself. What if she fell again? Seemed likely, given that she was basically balancing all of her weight on one leg. She could get hurt even more. She could get lost, and then he'd be looking for her and for Sam. He shook his head. "I'll go with you. Here. Lean on me."

She hooked her arm over his shoulders, but they quickly learned that they needed both arms to be free for balance while climbing through the brush. She let go and trailed him, leaning on trees as they passed them, hissing through her teeth against the pain. As they moved, her limp became less pronounced, but he could see by the set of her jaw and the sweat around her shirt collar that she was still in pain.

When he looked back at her worriedly, she gave a thin, encouraging smile and called out. "Sam? Sa-a-am?"

Jeremy squeezed his eyes shut and swallowed. Gratitude. It had been Laura's big thing. She was always better at it than he was. It wasn't that he wasn't grateful for what life had given him. It was just that he was always so caught up in daily minutiae, he didn't often focus on it. *God surprises you with little gifts all day long*, Laura used to say. *You just have to take the time to see them and be thankful for them.* After she died, he regretted all the time that he wasn't aware of his gratitude for her. And he worried that she didn't know he was grateful. But it was Laura—she knew just because that was who she was.

Little gifts. He very much doubted she'd meant someday a youth group leader would become that gift while hunting for their lost daughter, but the spirit of the phrase was the same. He'd worked very hard on learning to recognize and express his gratitude for Sam after Laura was killed. But he wasn't sure how much he could express right now.

The strange thing was, he thought it was possible that Whitney knew anyway.

So instead he just gave her a nod, cupped his hand around his mouth, and yelled. "Sam!"

Chapter Six

They determined that the rest area was above them, so they hiked to a spot where the mountain rose more gradually, even though it was taking them farther away from where they wanted to be. It was hard enough just walking, much less climbing, and there were areas below them where the hill steepened, where a wrong step could send them cascading down farther into who knew what, so Whitney didn't mind the extra walking. She felt guilty, like every second they spent worrying about her ankle was a second they weren't focusing on Sam. She wished more than anything that she hadn't fallen, a wish that had nothing at all to do with the throbbing in her ankle.

As they walked, they continued calling for Sam but never heard a reply. Whitney couldn't help thinking Sam could've taken a wrong step just as she had, and that she could be down the mountain, her injuries far greater than a wrenched ankle. Whitney didn't even want to think about the misfortunes that could be keeping Sam from answering their calls.

She could tell Jeremy was thinking the same things. And battling himself over it. He seemed to be holding his entire body tense like a clenched fist, his eyes darting everywhere at once, following every tiny sound that echoed around them. A few times, he glanced back at her, and every time she tried to offer him an encouraging smile, one that said, *All good back here*! She didn't need him worrying about her on top of worrying about Sam.

"She took the mountaineering safety course," Whitney said to Jeremy's back, trying to sound reassuring. "They all did."

"Two hours of videos," Jeremy responded, but it didn't seem acerbic or sarcastic so much as a lamentation.

"It was more than that," she countered.

"Yes, but we all watched the videos, and look where it got us," he said. "Rule number one, don't go up into a mountain forest if a storm is coming. Rule broken. Number two, don't split up. Rule broken. Rule number three, keep your eyes open so you don't get injured. Rule broken. Watch that spot right there." He pointed at a complexly interwoven series of ruts, then grabbed her elbow to help her get past the worst of it. "Not to mention all of my own personal rules. The most important rule, don't lose your daughter on a field trip." He seemed like he wanted to say more but thought better of it and held back.

Whitney wasn't sure how to take everything he'd

said. She couldn't blame him for venting, and even she wasn't sure how much of this disaster she would end up owning. Her guilt kept her from being irritated at him, even if he was being harsh.

Instead of responding, she simply plowed ahead with sweat sprouting on her forehead, even though the temperature had dropped. She told herself that as soon as she could see a sign of civilization, she would tell Jeremy to go on without her. She would give him the walkie and send Rob out to search with him.

But she couldn't see anything man-made yet. All she could see through the trees were gray clouds that had rolled in. How long had they been at this? *Time flies when you're falling down a mountain*, she thought deliriously.

She guessed by now, Rob and the kids had launched an all-out search party for them. She burned with embarrassment as she considered what mountaineering transgressions Rob would pile on. She felt like a big, fat failure. And if Sam turned out to be with the group, the failure would be even worse, because it would all have been for nothing.

Although, at the same time, it would be better, because Sam would be found.

Every few feet, they paused for Whitney to catch her breath and steel herself for more hiking, and for Jeremy to call out for Sam. In those moments, they pricked their ears for any voice or cry, but they never heard anything except the rustle of high branches as the wind picked up.

"Why…do you suppose…" Whitney said, the intensity of her breathing increasing as she climbed. "Why…aren't we…hearing *anybody*? Like…Rob and…the other kids…or other…hikers?"

Jeremy's steps seemed to slow, as if he hadn't considered this question before. "I don't know," he said. "Maybe they still haven't realized. We haven't been out here for that long. And the trail was pretty quiet."

But they both glanced to the sky, and Whitney knew he was thinking the same thing she had been thinking—that they'd been out here long enough to have made it back, and those youth group kids were not quiet at all. They'd been out there long enough for the sun and clouds to shift. More than enough time for Rob and the kids to reach the peak and realize that they'd reached it without a few members of their party.

Long enough for the cupcakes to be missed, if nothing else.

Only that thought made Whitney realize with a start that she'd left her pack on the ground by the bench at the rest area, her jacket with it. A new wave of humiliation washed over her. Of all of her mistakes, that was the most egregious. How hard was it to keep a pack on your back? Who would go into the woods without one?

Panic, she thought. *I was panicking, and people make avoidable errors when they're panicking.*

They got to a level ridge and paused, both of them breathing hard from the final few feet up the cliff, where it had felt like a ninety-degree incline. Whitney understood, after climbing up, that she would've never been able to stop her descent once gravity had kicked in. There was a definite drop-off, and the loose rocks had shuttled her right over it. She turned and gazed back to where she'd just been sitting against the tree. Her injuries could have been so much worse. In that regard, she was lucky. She needed to stay focused on the positives.

Positive thoughts breed positive outcomes, her mother used to say during hard times. Especially when Whitney was feeling sorry for herself.

Thank you, God, she thought, *for keeping me safe. Now, please keep Sam safe, too*.

But once again, she was distracted by the voices she did not hear. Was it a matter of time… Or a matter of distance?

"You don't think we're too far away from the rest area to hear them, do you?" she asked. They both scanned the forest around them. Whitney pricked up her ears for a laugh. Or a cry. Something. Anything. All she heard was wind and rustling leaves and birdsong.

"I don't think so," Jeremy said, but she could tell by the way his eyes shifted from tree to tree that he wasn't as confident about that as he wanted to seem. He pointed off to their left. "I think it's straight that direction."

To Whitney's memory, it seemed to be a slightly different direction, but she didn't want to argue. She was hardly crushing this mountaineering thing—who would want to trust her? Not even herself.

"Hey, um…" Jeremy studied the ground between

them. "I'm sorry for unloading on you earlier. Sam is everything to me. The thought of something happening to her is…" He trailed off, clenching his jaw so tight, Whitney worried he would crush his teeth to bits. "It's not an excuse, though. You didn't deserve that."

"I understand," she said. "No worries. Honestly." She reached over and patted his shoulder sympathetically. "We don't need to talk about it."

A low grumble rolled across the sky, and both of them looked upward. The clouds had not only shifted, but had darkened, and the forest was filling with shadows. It was beginning to look like Jeremy might have been right when he worried that the storm could arrive earlier than predicted.

"We should get moving," she said.

Jeremy nodded, but it was a doubtful nod, and a fearful one. He glanced at her leg. "Is your ankle—?"

"Right as rain," Whitney said, then cringed at her own word choice. *Right as the rain that's about to drench us both if we don't get walking.* Also, she could feel the swelling start to press her skin against the sides of her shoes. She wondered if he could tell, but refused to look at her ankle herself, for fear of drawing attention to it if he hadn't noticed.

Thunder groaned louder over their heads and they started moving, pushing a little faster than Whitney's ankle could go without a lot of protesting. Still, she kept her head down and kept her legs moving. One step, and then the next. And the next. *Go ahead and protest*, she thought. *We've got to do what we've got to do.*

The rain started slowly at first, heavy droplets splatting against the leaves above them. They couldn't feel or see them yet, and in some ways it felt like they were inside, the raindrops pounding on the roof. But soon enough, the drops picked up into a steady patter and the water finally broke through to the ground, the illusion gone. Whitney squinted against the rain, pushing forward and forward and forward, watching as dark dots of wetness bloomed on Jeremy's shoulders and upper back. The cool water felt good against her forehead at first, but soon turned cold as the rain and wind picked up speed.

They'd been walking for what seemed like forever. Whitney thought they may have gone even deeper into the forest, but it was impossible to tell. For all she knew, they'd been walking in circles this whole time.

No rest area. No Rob. No Sam.

She tipped her face to the sky, blinking as the rain stung her eyes. "Mom," she whispered. "Help me out a little, here? Which way do we go? God? I'll take a sign from you, too, if you'd like to send one."

Jeremy slowed to a stop. "What was that?"

"Nothing," Whitney said, sheepish. "I was just... talking. Kind of praying, I guess?" Although she tended to consider little side conversations like that to be more like check-ins than actual prayer.

"Huh. Good luck," he said, and then kept walking.

Whitney half jogged to catch up with him, wincing every step of the way. "What does that mean?" she asked.

"Nothing," he said. "Let's just keep going before this rain gets worse."

But to her, it wasn't nothing at all. Prayer was second nature to her. She didn't just do it—she relied on it. She might have pressed the issue, made him explain whatever it was that she'd heard behind that *huh*, but at that moment, Jeremy stopped short and spun in a circle. He threw his arms up, frustrated. "Are we going the right way?"

Whitney gazed around. Again, nothing had changed, except it was getting increasingly harder to see through the trees for the dark clouds.

"I don't know." She licked her lips. Her words felt swallowed up by the rain that was now pressing in on them sideways. She could feel it pricking the insides of her ears. "I thought it was that way, but everything looks the same to me now. I have no idea where we are." Admitting it aloud made it somehow seem more real. Like they were lost before, but now they were more lost, because it was spoken.

"Me, neither," Jeremy said, making the situation feel even more desperate.

Whitney felt the words in the pit of her stomach. They were lost now, just like Sam. Maybe they were lost *instead* of Sam. They had no way of knowing, until—unless—they got back to civilization. But for the first time, she began to wonder *if* they would get back to civilization. The gravity of the situation settled on her like a weight so heavy it nearly took her breath away.

She opened her mouth to ask Jeremy what he thought they should do next, but a clap of thunder, incredibly close and incredibly loud, pulled a short shriek out of her instead. The rain picked up—something that seemed impossible—and the first hailstones began to smack the rocks and trees around them. Whitney covered her head with her arms. What would they do if the hailstones got bigger? What if they got big enough to injure them?

Now, she thought. *Now is the time to send help, Mom. We're in big trouble. Because...we're lost.*

Chapter Seven

After the first boom of thunder, Jeremy knew he needed to take action. If there was anything he knew for sure, it was that where there was thunder, there was lightning. They couldn't just stand on a mountain in the middle of a rainstorm, waiting to be pummeled by electricity. And now hail. Perfect.

Although, he supposed, a good pummeling might be something he deserved. He knew before ever getting on this mountain that it was not a good idea, and he'd ignored his own instincts and endangered Sam. Why? Had losing Laura taught him nothing at all? And now, if he lost Sam… Well, he couldn't even really let himself think about that.

And to make it worse, he'd taken out his frustrations on Whitney. She didn't deserve it, and he knew that. His apology was thin, and he knew that, too. He knew Whitney hadn't meant to get hurt. He knew she was doing her best to keep up with him, to show a brave face. And he actually admired that about her.

But he was just so scared, he felt like he was about to blow.

In those early days after Laura's death, he'd been angry. The kind of angry where he almost didn't recognize himself. He seethed at other people's happiness, sneered at their shallow problems, wished the entire world would just go away and leave him with his grief. He was angry at the situation in general, and definitely angry at the man who killed his wife, but the thrust of his anger came after he learned that the man had come in through the unlocked back door after closing hours. Laura had been alone in her office, counting the cash drawers. How many times had he warned her about that, and how many times had she told him to stop worrying so much? He had never been so furious to be right in his entire life.

It had taken a long time and a lot of work to get past the anger, and when he did, he was hit with grief like a freight train, which only served to make him wish for the anger to return instead. All he could think was how he could never go through that again.

Now he was afraid they wouldn't find Sam, and he just might have to.

And then Whitney had to go and mention prayer, and it was just the wrong time.

He knew praying was Whitney's way of doing everything she could to help. But he also knew that saying a bunch of meaningless words—hopes, were really all they were—was not going to get them off this mountain, nor was it going to keep the rain away. Asking for protection was a waste of time when you were already in trouble. You had to protect yourself, and the ones you loved, period. At the very least, you had to protect the ones you were with.

Which, he had to recognize, was exactly what Whitney was trying to do. He might not agree with her methods, but he had to respect the sentiment behind them. He had to notice they had at least that much in common. Later. He would ponder hypocrisy when he was at home with his daughter and two cups of hot cocoa.

"Come on." He grabbed Whitney's hand and plunged deeper into the woods, into an area where the trees were clustered tighter. Since raiding his pack, he wasn't exactly sure what he had left in there, but he was fairly certain he had a few things that might be able to help them if things got really bad. Okay, worse than the already-really-bad that they were currently experiencing.

Whitney followed, willingly but still limping, reminding him to slow down. Her hand was cold; the temperature had dropped, and it was barely evening yet. He tried not to think what any of this could mean for poor Sam, if she was out in this. Was she going to get cold? Did she have something to warm her?

Don't think. Stay focused.

He found a spot, let go of Whitney's hand and dropped his pack on a nearby rock. There was another bang of thunder. She jumped. It was only then that Jeremy became really aware that Whitney was experiencing fear of her own. Of course she was.

"Do you think you can find some sticks?" Jeremy

asked. He felt his voice straining—he was having to yell over the sound of the storm. He couldn't tell if it had really started pouring that hard, or if it was just the sound of the rain hitting the trees that made it sound so. The water continually running into his eyes told him it was the former.

Whitney nodded and started combing the ground under the trees, while Jeremy opened his pack and shook out the tarp he'd left inside. It was the smaller of his tarps—the other was, maddeningly, still on the bus—but there were only two of them here, and if they huddled together, they would fit under it. He unfolded the tarp and pulled out the rope and utility knife that he'd also packed.

Quickly, as if he'd done it a thousand times before, he cut the rope in two, punched holes on each end of the tarp, ran the pieces of rope through the holes and secured them around the trunks of two trees. Instantly, the sound of the rain and hail grew louder as it thumped the plastic, which waved around in the wind like a flag.

Whitney came back with a handful of sticks, which Jeremy used to punch through the tarp and secure one side to the ground. Now they had a lean-to and could burrow back as far as they were able toward the side secured to the ground. Hopefully that would get them out of the worst of the storm.

"Get in, get in," he said, shooing Whitney under the shelter.

She sank to her hands and knees and crawled inside. Jeremy crawled in after her. They were both soaked, dripping, and Whitney was shivering hard, though he couldn't tell if it was from the rain, the cold or simply adrenaline.

The rain was still hitting them from the sides on huge gusts of wind that ripped down the mountain, but they were out from under the worst of it. Jeremy rooted around in his pack until his hands fell on the crinkly Mylar survival blanket that he'd thankfully not removed. He pulled it out and wound it around both of their shoulders, holding on to one end while Whitney clutched the other. She pulled herself into such a tight little ball, he wondered how she could be comfortable at all.

"I'm glad you knew how to do that," she said. The wind had freed much of her hair from its braids, and it clung to her face in little wet clumps. He had to fight the strange urge to brush them back with his fingers.

"I didn't," he said. "At least I didn't know that I did." He shifted his end of the blanket so that it was blocking the waves of sideways rain from getting to them. He was aware of his own legs aching from all the hiking. Hers must have been on fire.

A particularly strong gust hit them, pushing Jeremy so that his shoulder met Whitney's. He swallowed back the awkwardness and left it there for the warmth. Soon the blanket would be just as soaked as they were, and then what?

"Well, you have good instincts, then," she said. "I'd still be out there in the rain if you weren't here."

"You wouldn't be out here at all if I wasn't here," he said bitterly, the flood of guilt for his earlier outburst once again sweeping over him. He ground his teeth, wishing he'd said nothing. "You followed me. You didn't have to."

"I was looking for Sam," she said. "If you hadn't gone into the woods…"

But she didn't finish the sentence. Jeremy knew that was because it would be untrue of her to claim she would've gone into the woods without him. He was beginning to understand this woman could do many things, but one thing he suspected she couldn't do was lie. Not believably.

"Besides," she said. "You were worried about the storm from the beginning. We probably shouldn't have ever been on the mountain. *You* wouldn't be out here if it weren't for *me*. Or, well, us."

He shook his head. Being right about the rain was a victory he no longer wanted. "If it wasn't the storm, it would've been something else. I would have found any number of things to protect Sam from." He let out a sardonic grunt of laughter and waved a hand at the forest around them. "A lot of good that does, right? Here we are. All that protection, and my daughter is gone."

"She isn't gone," Whitney said. "You can't think that way."

"It's the only way I can think," he said. She blinked, and a hint of mascara imprinted itself on the tops of her cheeks. Long lashes. "All Sam has is me. I'm supposed to keep her safe. She trusts me. And I let her down."

Whitney shook her head. "You didn't know."

"But I did. I did know. I knew from the moment Laura…" He trailed off. He couldn't finish the sentence. It was too painful.

"Laura?" Whitney asked.

"My wife," he said. "She would have been as disappointed in me as I am right now."

"I'm sure that's not true. It was all an accident," Whitney said, her voice barely above a whisper. "And we'll find her. We will."

He held a hand out and was stung by a dozen speeding raindrops in seconds. "If she lives long enough to be found," he said.

"She will. She's a smart girl, and besides, God—"

But before she could finish her sentence, a powerful gust of wind ripped through them, first stealing one side of the tarp from its tree, leaving it blowing like a flag of surrender, and then ripping that away, too.

Whitney and Jeremy both jumped to their feet and ducked against the pelting rain, watching as their shelter blew away from them, down the mountain, only to get hung up on a low branch down below. Whitney clutched the survival blanket tightly and started toward the tarp, but Jeremy held her back.

"Leave it!" he yelled. And when he saw the confused look on her face, gestured toward what he'd seen when the first side had been ripped away. He pointed toward a nearby ridge. "A cave!"

Chapter Eight

It was a steep climb to the little cave, and as they got closer, Whitney could see it was little more than a depression where two mountains met, and that there were overgrown weeds in front of the entrance. She was surprised, honestly, that Jeremy had seen it at all.

Her ankle cried out with each step, but she clamped her mouth shut and kept going, the noise of crashing thunder distracting her from the pain. As they came out of the trees and the rain hit them unencumbered, the drops stung. Up here on the mountain, Whitney felt like she was actually inside the angry clouds, something she'd never considered before. She prayed harder than ever that Sam had found shelter or was still with Rob.

Finally, they reached the cave and crawled inside. It was deep enough to escape the rain, although not much deeper. Which was good, because she wouldn't have to worry about any animals fighting to protect their home. Thank God for small favors. She sat with the survival blanket balled up in her lap and scooted back as far as she could go against the rock to make space for Jeremy. He settled beside her with his head laid back against the rock and his legs kicked out in front of him. They were both soaked and gasping to catch their breath. Whitney was grateful to get out of the wind and hail, and grateful that the small space brought warmth and rest. She worked to spread out the blanket across her lap to give it a chance to dry. They sat quietly for what seemed like forever, as the storm raged outside.

Whitney thought about all the things Jeremy had said to her. All the blame, all the guilt—how he'd lashed out at her, but then ultimately took it all on himself. And then there was the weird thing about her praying. No doubt about it, Jeremy was a complicated man.

Whitney didn't know Jeremy well; she only knew that he was a widower, incredibly dedicated to his daughter, Sam. Whitney had often observed his interactions with Sam and found them to be tender and caring in a way that warmed her heart. She was sure there was more of a story behind his wife's death, but every effort she'd made to engage Jeremy in conversation in the past was met with vault-like privacy. Now, more than ever, she realized that his fierce silence was probably a simple matter of protection. He knew his own complexity, and he didn't want to burden others with it. Whitney found something appealing about that.

Whitney's own father had been a brooder. He

would sit in silence for hours, go about his work without a word, watch TV without speaking, eat dinner without expressing a single opinion. Just a slight smile curving at the corners of his lips when he watched her clown around, nodding intently as he listened to her jabber on and on.

As a little girl, she'd been perplexed by this. She and her mother talked about everything. All the time. When they were in the same room, there was scarcely a silent moment between them. She once asked her mother about her father's curious behavior, and that was the first time she heard the phrase, "Still waters run deep."

He's a wonderful man, Whitney, her mom said. *He's just different from you and me. You'll find in life that sometimes the people who talk all the time say nothing at all, and the ones who are quiet say everything that needs to be said.*

In time she learned to navigate the silence, to understand that not everyone spoke their minds at all times. Not everyone wore their feelings on their sleeves. This made it easier to sit in Jeremy's silence now. It was actually, after a while, comfortable.

She watched as he shifted, sat forward and peered out into the curtain of rain. His jaw tightened and relaxed, tightened and relaxed. He was feeling anxious for Sam again.

Whitney reached over and touched his shoulder.

"She's a smart girl," she said. "I'm sure she's found safety." She wasn't sure. In fact, her insides were rolling with uncertainty, but she sensed Jeremy needed someone to believe in Sam right now, believe in possibility, even if the possibility wasn't great.

"She's smart," he agreed, nodding. "Smart enough to not go missing to begin with."

"She made a mistake," Whitney said. "It was overconfidence, maybe."

"She was led to believe this trip was safe." Whitney opened her mouth to defend the decision to hike the mountain, but he continued. "I led her to believe it. She never had any reason to doubt it. I led her to think I had everything covered, because I always do."

"You did. You do. You couldn't have seen this coming."

He faced Whitney, and she fully saw the anguish. "But I did see it coming. I knew this could happen. It's my job to see these things coming. Literally. I've always protected her, always predicted what could happen and stopped it before it did. Sam had every reason to trust me, and I betrayed that trust. Again."

His voice broke on the word *again*, and Whitney's heart squeezed. She didn't know what to say. He seemed to be holding back something, and she didn't know him well enough to press for more information. Even though she was so curious.

A crack of lightning struck the ground close to them, lighting up the cave as if someone had pointed a spotlight inside. It seemed the whole world shivered, and Whitney was struck by the knowledge she'd been sheltered—literally—from rainstorms all her life. Lightning was always something far away, the kind of danger that doesn't feel real. She had never been so up close and personal to a lightning strike. It seemed like a silly thing to be worried about, until you were right up on it and could feel its power. Out here on the mountain, she felt bare and vulnerable. If the lightning wanted to find her here—turn that power into actual danger—she had no way of stopping it. She was small and helpless against this side of nature. Her teeth chattered.

What she wouldn't give to be at home in her fluffy white robe, watching streaks of water pour down the bedroom window. Mesmerized by the patterns the rain made against the glass.

Or better yet, watching the rain from over a shared plate of pad thai, laughing with her mom about shopping antics they'd had earlier in the day and planning their second wave. Her heart ached at the thought.

She wondered if her mom knew exactly how this was going to go—if she had an inside line on whether or not Whitney would come out of this predicament alive. Maybe the little woodpecker had been sent for a bit of comfort, after all. Whitney liked the idea—she liked to envision the bird with Sam, the two of them literally weathering the storm together.

Silly, Whitney thought. *You're just being silly now.* Yes, but it was the kind of silliness that allowed her to remain calm, even though her insides were quivering and flinching every time a flash of electricity lit up their world.

After a few minutes of watching in silence, Jeremy shimmied out of his backpack and opened it. He pulled out a bottle of water and handed it to her.

"Thirsty?"

It seemed impossible that she would be, given she was soaked to the bone from all the water raging just outside, but she was thirsty. She took the bottle, cracked it open and took a sip.

"I've been trying not to think about it, since I left my pack behind." She shivered. "And my jacket."

"That blanket is warm. And waterproof, so it will dry quickly. If you'd rather, you can wear my jacket." He dug around in the pack, but Whitney put a hand out to stop him.

"The blanket will be fine. Really. But thank you. You're very kind to offer." They held each other's gaze for a moment before he went back to his bag.

"I have four bottles of water, so we should be okay," he said. "And a handful of food. You hungry?"

She was, but she shook her head. Food could wait until she was hungrier. She took another small sip of water, then handed the bottle back to him. He took a drink and offered it again, but she waved it away. He recapped the bottle, then leaned against the wall, his shoulder once again butting up against hers. He rubbed his forehead, then let his hand drop into his lap.

"When Laura—my wife—died, I made a promise. To Sam, but more to Laura, really. I promised that I would take care of Sam. Do everything in my power to protect her and to raise her the way Laura and I had planned." He licked a drip of rainwater that had cascaded down his face onto his lips. "And I meant it. Everything I did, and everything I do, I think about

how Laura would do it, what she would think. At first,
I questioned every single decision I made, no matter
how small. *Should I take a shower now or wait until
she's asleep? If I wait until she's asleep and someone
breaks into the house, what then? Should I make peas
or corn to go with dinner? Which is healthier? What
was the last vegetable I gave her? Is it balanced? Am
I feeding her enough? Am I feeding her too much? Too
little sleep, too much sleep? Should I make her do her
homework as soon as she gets home from school or
let her watch TV for a while first to decompress?* On
and on and on. I was so scared I would fail. It's still
my biggest fear, really. Losing someone precious to
you shakes up everything you think. Everything you
ever thought. Even things you used to be confident
about." He shrugged and shook his head. "I know
people think I'm overprotective. *Mr. No-No.* And I
don't like it, but I'm that way for a reason. I have to
be. I'm all she has."

Whitney didn't know what to say. She fixed her
gaze straight ahead so he wouldn't feel like she was
staring at him. Her gut sank at hearing him say *Mr.
No-No.* It hadn't occurred to her that he might know
about the nickname, and how it would make him feel.
She tried to focus instead on the warmth of his shoulder against hers, a feeling that was surprisingly pleas-
ant. She welcomed it.

He chuckled, as if someone had told a joke only he
could hear. "You know, I can hear her?" He glanced
at Whitney. "Laura. I can hear her. I mean, I hear her
all the time. But I can hear her *right now,* like she's

always standing behind me, telling me what to do. Or, more often, what to stop doing."

"Stop doing? Like what?"

"Stop worrying," he said, his voice going higher as if to mimic his wife's voice. "Stop thinking about all the bad things that could go wrong all the time. Stop being such a risk assessor." He chuckled again, but softer this time.

"I know exactly what you mean," Whitney said. "I lost my mom a few months ago. I hear her all the time. Well, and see her, actually. Not physically. More like in my mind's eye."

"I'm sorry." He glanced at her again. "Was the loss sudden?"

Whitney nodded, surprising herself. She hadn't really talked about her mother's death to anyone. People knew, of course. She missed a lot of work during those first few weeks while she tried to iron out all the details of stopping the wheels of someone's life. A house to sell, tons of belongings to get rid of, keepsakes to protect, phone calls to make, paperwork to file—the list was long and arduous, especially for an only child.

But even when she came back to work, nobody asked questions, which Whitney appreciated. It was mentally exhausting, and most people found grief and the exhaustion that followed to be too heavy and awkward to be around. They couldn't handle it. Almost as if they were afraid it was contagious.

And when she was away from the emotional tasks of burying her mother, she didn't even want to think about what was happening in her life, how with both parents gone, she was now an orphan. How the only person who knew her entire life story was gone. She certainly didn't want to talk about it. So she never volunteered the information. Her grief was between her, her mother and God. In that way—which she'd never before considered—maybe she and Jeremy were alike.

She was overcome with a feeling she could tell him anything, and he would just get it. She wouldn't need to go into any detail that she didn't want to—he would be able to fill in those gaps himself. She could share the hard things without sharing the hardest things.

And part of her thought that maybe sharing the hardest things with him wouldn't be that bad, anyway. Listening to him talk about his wife, laying himself bare, touched her. This was a side of Jeremy she was pretty sure nobody in the youth group had seen. It took courage for him to tell her these things. She wanted to give back. She wanted to share with him, too.

"A few months ago. Totally unexpected. Although I don't know what that means, really. Who expects someone they love to die? Feels like it would always be unexpected."

"You got that right," he said, but his voice was so quiet, Whitney wondered if he was really saying it to himself.

"Anyway, we were texting each other, and then she stopped responding. It was getting kind of late, so I didn't think anything of it. Sometimes she fell asleep on the couch." Whitney swallowed against the guilt that filled her every time she thought about her dismissal of her mother's sudden loss of contact. If she'd followed up immediately, would she have been able to save her? The doctors said no, but there would always be that question in the back of Whitney's mind.

"But the next day, when she didn't answer my texts all day long, I went over there. She was on the couch, like I thought. But she wasn't asleep. She'd had a stroke."

"I'm sorry," Jeremy repeated softly. She could tell he was looking at her, but she'd never told anyone any of this before, so she was afraid if she looked at him, she would crack. She kept her eyes on the rocky cave ground, by her feet.

"She looked very peaceful, though. And she was still holding her phone. My text was pulled up." There was something about that fact that comforted Whitney. *I love you* hadn't been the last thing she said to her mother. In fact, the last thing she'd said was, *Like with a toothbrush?* Not exactly earth-shattering or heartfelt. Just another conversation about nothing, like the billion they'd had before. But it was the fact that she was, in some way, with her mother at her last moment that kept her from losing it completely.

"Anyway," Whitney said. "It's like she's always around, even though she's not. Which is good, because at first I was so scared I would forget her. But it also makes it hard to heal, you know?"

He nodded. "Yeah. And I also understand about the fear of forgetting. For a long time, I wrote down everything. Every time a memory or detail would pop into my head, I'd put it on paper. Sam may not remember much about her someday. It's my job to keep her memory alive. At first, that felt like a monumental job."

"Do you mind me asking…?" Whitney said, leaving the question open.

"Armed robbery. She was shot in her office at work," he said.

Whitney sucked in a breath. Of all the ways she'd imagined his wife to have gone, that brutal way of going was not even on her radar of possibilities. "I'm so sorry," she breathed, placing her hand over her heart. "I had no idea."

"I wasn't exactly expecting it to happen, either," he said. "But it did. And we moved on. You have to."

Whitney remembered how the world seemed to stop that day she found her mother on the sofa, the TV still turned on, a game show studio audience laughing in the background. In those first few foggy days, she had no idea how life would start up again. She didn't think moving on would be possible. But then she remembered her mother going forward after Whitney's father died. She'd cried, she'd raged, she'd bought a lot of junk food. But then she gathered herself together and got going again. She didn't have a choice. Because she had Whitney to take care of.

Whitney imagined this was how Jeremy felt after his wife died. He didn't have a choice but to move on. Because he had Sam.

The storm wasn't letting up at all, but the lightning

had gotten farther away, the thunder less bone rattling. Whitney still felt too close to the storm, but with the cave blocking the wind and the rain, and the heat of Jeremy's side next to hers, she started to warm up. The throbbing in her ankle had ebbed some, and she found herself getting sleepy. She glanced at her phone to see the time—the darkness of the clouds made it feel like midnight, but it was barely nine o'clock.

"We've been walking around these woods for hours," she mused.

Jeremy glanced at her phone. "So has Sam," he said. "Too many hours."

Outside, there was a howl of wind and the crack of a tree trunk. Whitney and Jeremy both winced, peering out of their cave to find the falling tree, but they couldn't see it. Whitney's heart ached for Jeremy and all the things he wasn't saying. Every hour that Sam was gone was another hour of lost time. She hoped Sam was staying put, wherever she was, and not getting farther away by the minute.

"God will take care of her," she said, mostly to herself.

But Jeremy made the *huh* noise again.

"What?" she asked.

"God hasn't exactly *taken care of her* so far," he said.

"I'm sure that's not true," Whitney said. "She has you."

"But she doesn't have her mother. Look what she's gone through under God's watch. Your God has let her suffer an awful lot."

"But she has a father who will do anything for her," Whitney said. "God has done that, too."

"Believe what you want. All I'm saying is I don't know what I believe anymore."

"If you don't mind my asking, why are you leading a youth group, then?" Whitney asked, stunned, thinking that belief in God would sort of be a prerequisite for the job title. In fact, she wasn't exactly sure what to do with this information. Did Pastor Penny need to know one of her youth group leaders didn't believe?

"Because Sam believes," he said. "At least, I think she does. We don't talk about it."

"Maybe you should," Whitney said. "It doesn't hurt to talk."

"You wouldn't like what I have to say," Jeremy said. "I'm there because Sam has friends there and she feels safe there. I do it for her. If she believes, I let her."

Hopefully that will be enough, Whitney thought, but her heart still felt heavy. She didn't understand how he could go through life with that view. But she knew it wasn't her place to argue with him, and that it would be a fruitless argument anyway. She understood how someone who had gone through what he'd gone through would feel soured against God. And she understood that he needed to come to his own realizations on his own time.

But his confession was a conversation ender, for sure. Whitney didn't regret sharing what she'd shared with him. She just didn't know how to continue sharing when her heart ached for the empty state of his.

After a while, Whitney's eyes started to grow heavy again, and this time she didn't have the will to keep herself from falling into a tunnel of sweet darkness where there was no lost child, no storm and—she was reluctant to admit this—she wasn't lost in the woods herself.

She felt her head bob with her chin dipping to her chest, and then bob the other way to bump against the rock wall behind her. Finally, she tipped it sideways, too tired to register that she'd laid it on Jeremy's shoulder. Too far gone to correct herself or feel embarrassed.

Almost too far gone to hear him say, "Trust me, I wish I could believe."

And completely out when she muttered the word *woodpecker* in response to a question that was never asked.

Chapter Nine

Whitney startled awake and came to in slow confusion. She looked blankly at the walls surrounding her and the rock floor beneath her and especially at the head of the man next to her, which had been leaning ever so lightly against her own. It took her a moment to piece together who she was leaning against, where they were and why.

Cave. Jeremy. Lost in the Ozark Mountains.

It wasn't the rock walls or the hard floor or the man that had awakened her, though. Nor was it the sun beaming into the cave in bright stripes of warmth, cutting across her eyelids.

She'd been awakened by a noise.

Woodpecker? she thought, ridiculously. What were the odds the sound of a bird's knocking would pull her out of sleep two mornings in a row? It was definitely a sound that had awakened her. She was sure of it.

She heard the sound again. But it wasn't a bird.

It was a cry. A child's cry. For help.

Sam.

Whitney jerked upright, forcing Jeremy's head to drop forward. He, too, sat up straight, but he seemed to have none of the confusion that Whitney did.

"Sam?" he rasped, springing forward onto his hands and knees so he was hanging out of the cave opening. "Is that…?" He glanced at Whitney just as another cry rang out. "It's Sam!" he said. He barreled forward out of the cave, leaving everything inside behind.

Whitney went into overdrive as she followed him, not remembering until she began to speed down the uneven, steeply sloped ground beneath her that her ankle had been injured the day before. As was often the case with injuries, the pain was worse than when it happened.

She made an *oof* noise but clamped her lips down on the end of it so Jeremy wouldn't hear her. He had paused and was waiting for her, but she could feel his impatience, and she couldn't blame him for it.

The cry came again. Whitney waved Jeremy off.

"I'm fine. It's better," she said, through gritted teeth. "Let's go!"

He seemed to think it over for just a moment, evaluating Whitney's honesty, but when another cry came, he sprang to life.

"Sam!" he shouted, his voice laced with anguish. "We hear you! Stay where you are! Keep calling!"

She searched her waistband for the walkie-talkie and, not finding it, went back to the cave. It was lying on the floor where she'd been sitting. She grabbed it and pressed the button on the side.

"Rob?" she said. "Can you hear me? It's Whitney." She listened, but got nothing other than frustrating static. She twisted the dial to change signal channels and tried again, and then again. "Rob? Rob?" She grunted with frustration as she stuffed the radio into her waistband and set off after Jeremy, grinding her teeth every time she took a step.

Her ankle was swollen. She could feel the edges of her shoe rub against it. But every time it threatened to distract her, Sam's cry would pierce the air again, and Whitney would be reenergized to charge through the woods behind Jeremy. As the cries got closer, she found herself being aware of her own issues less and less. Could it really be Sam? What a miracle!

When Whitney finally caught up with Jeremy, she found him standing once again at the edge of the cliff she'd only a day before fallen over. His head was cocked, listening for Sam's cries.

"Sam?" Whitney called. They'd both heard it, so she knew it wasn't her imagination.

Sam called back, something unintelligible. The sound was definitely coming from below them, but they could not see her at the bottom of the cliff. Jeremy gave Whitney a questioning look and she nodded. *Yes*, she tried to convey with her eyes, somehow just knowing he would understand her, *I can get back down there.*

Carefully, as careful as they could be with such excitement coursing through them, they picked their way back to a flatter area, where they could get down the cliff without slipping or free-falling, although Whitney had a feeling if she weren't with him, Jeremy might have jumped off that cliff to get to his daughter faster.

Jeremy scrambled down roots and rocks while Whitney braced herself a little more cautiously, always keeping an ear out for Sam and an eye out for Jeremy when he got too far ahead.

Finally, on flatter land again, they began to hear actual words.

"Daddy? Help!"

"Sam! I'm here!" Jeremy called back, his voice an emotional cocktail that Whitney couldn't quite pinpoint. "I'm coming! Stay put!"

"Keep calling, Sam!" Whitney said, as she and Jeremy began to frantically search the area. It sounded like Sam was always right over their shoulder, or right behind them, but they couldn't see her anywhere. Her cries seemed to be coming from everywhere at once.

"I'm right here!" she called. Whitney could hear hysteria edging the girl's voice.

"Where, honey?" Jeremy called. The muscles on his shoulders were so tight under his damp shirt, Whitney could make them out. His fists were clenched, as if he were preparing to fight the woods to reclaim his daughter. Whitney could almost feel his effort at remaining calm, which was hard for her to do, with Sam sounding so small and scared. She could only imagine how difficult it was for him. "Describe it. We can't see you!"

"Down here!" she called. "I'm in a hole!"

Whitney and Jeremy exchanged glances again. *In a hole?* They turned their attention downward, scanning the area, and followed Sam's voice until they saw it at exactly the same time—another bed of loose rock, just like the rock Whitney had slid on, that dumped into a narrow crevasse below them. Another two steps and they would have fallen into it.

When they inched to the edge and crouched to peek over the side, Sam's tired, dirt-smudged face, gazed back at them.

"Daddy!" she cried, her face crumpling into a sob that tore Whitney's heart in two. Somehow it reminded her of her own sobs on the evening her mother had died—once she'd gotten home and the reality of the loss fell upon her in full force. A face-in-the-pillow, breath-stealing cry. A cry for all the things she missed already, and all of the things that she knew she was going to miss. A cry that pounded inside her chest, trying to get out in gales stronger than her body could accommodate, knocking against her ribs, knocking, knocking, knocking like… Like a woodpecker?

Whitney! Let go of the bird!

She saw Jeremy swallow as he took in the situation. The tears that had sprung to her eyes were not in his. Instead, there was desperation, determination and a hint of relief. They'd found her. Now they just had to get to her.

Jeremy dropped to his belly and reached toward his daughter. She reached for his hands, and Whitney had a thought that it might have made a beautiful photograph if the situation were different—father and daughter stretching to cling to each other like a modern-day version of the *Creation of Adam* painting. The stretch was natural and trusting, as if they had been reaching for each other since the day of her birth. And in some ways, Whitney was sure, they had been. They both grunted in effort and frustration as the tips of their fingers waved near each other but never quite touched. Not even a graze.

Sam scrambled against the side of the crevasse, trying to get as high as she could, but the rocks gave and she fell back, letting out a howl of anguish and defeat. Jeremy's head drooped forward, as well, and he panted against the rocky crevasse wall.

"Sam? Honey? It's okay," Whitney called, trying to reassure them both. She knew that Sam's cries would rattle Jeremy. And she knew that she was trained to be a reassuring, steady presence in times of emergency. "We'll get you out, but you have to stay calm."

"Let's try again," Jeremy said, scooting so his top half was even farther over the edge of the crevasse, the toes of his shoes digging into the rock and earth as he tried to maintain his balance. Sam was not a big girl, but she would be big enough to topple someone over an edge if the weight distribution was off.

Whitney glanced around for the rope they'd lost to the storm last night, or anything else that might help ground and steady him. She was just about to hold his feet herself when their fingers touched and Sam fell backward again.

Jeremy thumped the ground with his fist and growled.

"Is there anything in your pack that could help?" she asked.

Jeremy paused to think and then shook his head slowly. "I emptied it on the bus, remember?"

"You had that rope—"

"It was the only one I had."

"Maybe it's around here somewhere," she said, though she knew she had already scanned the area and hadn't seen it. She distinctly remembered seeing the rope fluttering in the wind off the corner of the tarp as it blew away. It was likely wrapped around a tree much farther down the mountain. "You're only a couple of inches short of reaching her. If we could secure your feet..." Whitney trailed off, an idea brewing.

"The rescue blanket," Jeremy said, reeling with ideas. "We could twist it into—but, no, what would we tie it to? It wouldn't be long enou—"

"Me!" Whitney said, the plan clear in her mind. "You can secure me. I don't think I'm strong enough to hold your feet, but you might be able to hold mine."

He seemed unsure, but Sam gave out another pitiful cry that moved him. "You're sure? What about your ankle?" he asked.

"It's fine. Really."

"What if I drop you?"

Whitney met his eye, feeling there was something—some element of trust that she'd never felt before with a man—passing between them. "You won't." She truly believed that.

She got down on her hands and knees. "Okay, Sam, I want you to grab my wrists, not my hands. And I'll grab yours. And then when I pull you up, use your feet to climb." She patted the rocky side of the crevasse. Now that she was closer, she could see Sam's head wasn't smeared with dirt, but with mostly dried blood. She wondered if Jeremy had seen it.

Sam sniffled and nodded. Her eyes were wide and wet and hopeful. *Please, God*, Whitney thought. *Give me the strength to get her out of there*. Then, feeling Jeremy's hands clasp around her ankles, revised, *Give us the strength. Together*.

Whitney lowered herself flat on her belly and inched so that her hips hinged over the ledge, which allowed her to lower her top half fully into the crevasse, getting much closer to Sam. If Jeremy gave way now, she would fall headfirst into the rocks. Or into Sam. Or both. She briefly squeezed her eyes shut to garner strength, then reopened them and, with a breath, reached toward the girl, stretching as far as she could go.

Sam reached upward, and after a couple of close misses, their hands clasped and then inched their way to each other's wrists. Whitney squeezed with everything she had.

"Got her!" Whitney yelled, and she felt Jeremy's hands tighten over her ankles in preparation. "Okay, Sam, you've gotta climb and pull like you're doing a pull-up."

"But I can't do a pull-up," Sam whined.

"If you try, that will be good enough," Whitney said. "But you have to try."

Sam started scrambling against the rock, her elbows bending slightly, and at first Whitney thought the weight of the little girl was going to pull her over the edge after all. She tensed her arm muscles so hard the felt like they would pop out of her skin and yanked upward.

"Pull me back!" she yelled. Jeremy's hands tightened even more and he tugged so that she slid backward just a couple inches. Whitney felt rock and grit scrape against her knees, her thighs, her belly and eventually her arms, as Jeremy tugged her one way and Sam's weight pulled the other. She'd never heaved so mightily against—or for—anything. But suddenly what had seemed a hopeful what-if was now the only important thing in this world, success so close that failure was no longer an option. Whitney was going to get Sam out of this hole in the ground, or she was going to fall in trying.

When she finally got to a place of equilibrium, she bent her knees and scooted herself backward and backward until Sam, whose hands were slipping down Whitney's wrists to her hands and eventually to the tips of her fingers, was close enough to grasp the edge of the crevasse.

"Help me," Whitney cried, and while she thought it was possible that she'd been talking aloud to God, it was Jeremy who jumped to action, springing forward and grabbing one of Sam's arms with both hands just as Sam's grip fell away entirely.

Sam cried out and Jeremy grunted as the weight of his daughter swung from his grasp alone, pulling him forward toward the crevasse.

"Reach up! Reach!" Whitney cried, and Sam held up her other, freely swinging hand. Whitney grasped Sam's forearm tight, and without a word, she and Jeremy tugged with everything they had. Sam's feet scratched and flailed against the rock face, and then she was up, falling on the ground next to Whitney, who'd flopped onto her back with the exertion.

Whitney gasped for breath, her muscles tingling, her eyes watering, and her ankle feeling hot points of pain where Jeremy's hands had been digging into it. She was aware of Sam's cries muffled by Jeremy's shirt, and his own hoarse breaths that sounded suspiciously like cries, but in the moment, she was transfixed by the trees and sky and the pebbles pressing into her back and the waves of relief that flooded her, the only thought in her mind a repetition: *Thank you, thank you, thank you.*

Chapter Ten

There was bravery and there was selflessness, and Jeremy was aware of both as he breathed in his daughter's scent, his fingers clawing into her back as if someone were going to tear her away from him at any moment. If they did, he would fight them off with his two bare hands, he knew that much. He would almost welcome the opportunity.

What he'd been surprised by was this new knowledge that Whitney might fight right alongside him.

Maybe she hadn't been aware of how far over the ledge she'd been dangling. Maybe she hadn't noticed when twice his sweaty hand slipped from her ankle—which was hugely swollen and very black-and-blue, he'd noted—and he'd had to readjust. Maybe she didn't feel the earth scraping her as he yanked her up, probably too quickly in his haste to save his daughter, and maybe she was unaware that he'd let go of her ankle just a split second before she'd called for him to.

Brave. Selfless.

For another person's child. Who did something like that?

He remembered an insurance claim he'd worked on a couple years before. A man had been in a store and had seen a shelf teetering over a little boy. He'd jumped in at the last second just as the weighty metal shelf had fallen. The boy had been scraped up from the rain of objects that had fallen off of the shelf, but had been missed by the shelf itself. Instead, it had landed on the man, crushing the hand that had caught it.

The man, who just happened to be passing by the right place at the wrong time, had lost his hand.

The boy was a stranger.

At the time, reviewing that claim, Jeremy had wondered who would do such a thing—be so self-sacrificing for someone they didn't know. Someone else's child.

Peering over his daughter's heaving shoulder at Whitney, who lay, completely spent, on her back, catching her breath, he thought, *This woman would,* and was overcome with gratitude. And also a pang of knowledge that maybe it wasn't just him and Sam against the world as he'd always seen it. Maybe there'd been allies all along and he'd been too caught up in his own seclusion to notice them.

Sam sobbed for a good long while and Jeremy simply held her. He knew his daughter enough to know that she didn't like to be coddled, but when she was broken, she needed his attention. She needed to be surrounded by him. He was her safe place, which made him ache again for letting her down, letting her get lost during this hike.

When she finally pulled away, he placed his hands gently on her cheeks and studied her.

"You're bleeding," he said, touching the dried blood that stained the side of her face. He could see the source of the blood—a goose egg high up on the right side of her temple, bruised and split, seeping. She also had a scrape along one side of her face, as if she'd skidded on the rock. He worried that might have happened when they pulled her up, but it, too, was dried. "What happened?"

Sam raised a hand to touch the wound on her head, but instead of touching it, her fingers lingered around it as if the pain could be felt in the disrupted air. Sometimes pain was just that way. You didn't need to actually be in it to know it was there and to feel it all the same.

"I hit my head," she said. "It really hurt."

"Why didn't you yell?" he asked. "We were calling for you all day yesterday. Trying to find you."

She winced. "At first, everything got really fuzzy, and when I tried yelling I would get dizzy and feel like I was going to throw up."

"But you didn't pass out?" Whitney asked. Jeremy remembered that Whitney was a nurse and was pretty sure that this question was part evaluation.

"I don't think so," Sam said. "And I thought I could hear you, but you weren't very loud. And then the storm came and I couldn't hear you at all." Her face crumpled and she started to cry again. Jeremy wrapped her back up in his arms. "The hail hurt. And it was cold."

"I'm sure you were really scared," he said. "But we're here now."

Whitney had sat up and scooted close to them. She reached over and rubbed Sam's back lightly. "And we're going to get you out of here. Are you injured anywhere else?"

Sam shook her head miserably. "But I kind of peed my pants."

Jeremy chuckled, giving her another hug. "We don't care about that. Pretty sure Whitney peed her pants, too. Don't tell her I noticed."

"Did not!" Whitney lightly slapped at Jeremy's arm, but he'd already gotten the desired result of Sam's giggle. "What were you doing way out here, anyway?"

"The line for the bathroom was really long and I had to go super bad," Sam said. "So I just went around back because it seemed faster. And I know we're always supposed to go with a partner, but Lily was sick, and I figured I would only be a few minutes and would come right back and nobody would notice. But I was afraid people could see, so I kept going until I couldn't see anyone anymore. Which was dumb, I know. I'm really sorry, Daddy."

"Not dumb, but maybe not the best plan in the world," Jeremy said, too relieved to have found her, to hear the word *Daddy* to be angry at how she got lost in the first place. And, for a change, too relieved to be angry at himself for letting her get lost. *But we will talk. Later. We will have discussions about safety. And then more discussions.*

"And when you went to go back to the rest area, all the trees looked the same to you, didn't they?" Whitney asked softly. "That happened to us, too." Jeremy picked up on the quick glance she gave him, and he wasn't sure if the glance was meant to convey a message to him, or to let him know that she'd understood his.

"Yeah." Sam squeezed her eyes shut and two fat tears tumbled down her cheeks. "I must have gone the wrong way or something. But I could still hear people talking, so I tried to go toward the sound, but it only ever got farther away. Like the sound was moving or something."

"Why didn't you call out then?" Jeremy asked. "We were probably already looking for you."

"Because I didn't want to get in trouble," Sam said, her chin quivering, something that always brought Jeremy to his knees. He hated that chin quiver and would do just about anything to stop it. "I thought if I could just get back to the rest stop, nobody would ever know I was missing."

"And if the group was gone…?"

She gave an ashamed shrug to her lap. "I would've pretended you left me in the bathroom."

"I see," Jeremy said. He supposed he sounded firm, but in that moment, he truly didn't feel it. He didn't have an interest in making Sam learn a lesson. He was certain she'd already learned any lesson he would be trying to impart.

"So I got scared and started running toward the voices. And then all of a sudden, I couldn't hear people anymore. And then I slipped on these stupid rocks and fell into a hole." She listlessly scooped up a handful of rocks and tossed them into the crevasse, then turned her big, round eyes to Jeremy's. "I'm sorry, Daddy. You told me to always stay with Lily, and I didn't."

Jeremy's heart squeezed as he pulled her back into a hug. "It's okay, Sam. You didn't mean for this to happen." He felt his own eyes prickle with tears. "You're safe, and we're going to get you home, and that's all that matters." He pulled her back to arm's length and studied the wound on her head. "Are you in a lot of pain?"

"Not really."

"Are you cold?" Whitney asked.

"I was last night, but not anymore," Sam said. "But I'm thirsty."

"We have water in the cave," Whitney said. "I'll go get it." And without waiting for Jeremy to argue, she got to her feet and limped back up the mountain toward their hidey-hole. He could feel Sam taking him in as he watched Whitney go, his mind swirling with an admiration that seemed to spring up out of nowhere.

At first when he'd realized they were lost and she was injured, she had felt like a liability. Now he was consumed with gratitude that she was there with them. Comforted.

He quickly turned his attention back to Sam. "I left my backpack in the cave," he said."

"Where is it?" she asked. "What cave?"

He scooted so that, together, they could see the dimple in the steep hill where he and Whitney had weathered the storm. Whitney was making good time, even though her uneven tread had gotten more pronounced, almost like a lurch. Jeremy had the brief thought that maybe she'd been hiding the truth from him about how her ankle felt, but now that she thought she was out of sight, was allowing herself to feel the pain. He pointed.

"That little hole?" Sam asked.

"Yep."

"You stayed in it together? How big is it?"

"Big enough," he answered, trying not to remember the feeling of Whitney's head lightly resting on his shoulder or hear the sound of her soft breath as he sank into sleep. Trying not to recall the comfort of that feeling, which he hadn't had since Laura died. Trying not to focus on how right it felt, how safe, the two of them in that cave together. She'd shared with him, someone she hardly knew, about the most difficult parts of her life. But, more strangely, he'd shared his with her. Not only had he never done that before, but he'd never even considered that he might.

"Will we all three fit in it?"

That, he didn't want to think about. And not only because he'd come to think of the cave as a private space—which was a feeling that was so far out of nowhere, he almost couldn't process it—but because they would only need it to be big enough for three if they were out here for another night, and if he had anything to say about it, they most definitely would not be. He couldn't even allow the possibility.

They watched in silence as Whitney made her way up the steep slope and then crawled into the cave. Soon after, his pack was pushed out into the open and she reappeared, balancing most of her weight on her good foot as she pulled herself to standing.

By the time she got back to them, she was pale and sweating.

"Here you go," she said, handing the pack to Jeremy. Their eyes lingered a little too long, and once again he felt as if they were exchanging a message in silence. *You okay? Yeah, I'm fine.* How was it that he could suddenly communicate this way with her?

The only other person in the world whom he could do that with was Laura. They were masters at it. They had their *Scold her before you laugh* look when Sam did something inappropriate but a little funny, their *Let's get out of here* look when they were bored or uncomfortable at a gathering, their look when they knew something nobody else in the room knew. Not only was she the only one he had that with, she was the only one he ever *wanted* to have that with.

No, he decided. Two looks with Whitney was not at all the same as what he had with Laura. They were coincidences. Flukes. Anomalies. That was it.

Sam had already unzipped the pack and was digging through it eagerly. "What happened to all your stuff?" she asked, and Jeremy had another pang of regret at having emptied his pack on the bus. He'd only had four waters to start, and he and Whitney had drained half of one of them already. The fact that she hadn't asked for more, even though her lips looked cracked and dry and she was surely spent from rescuing Sam and hiking to the cave and back, did not go unnoticed.

"We lost a tarp and some rope in the storm last night," he said. "But there are water bottles in there. And some food."

But not enough of either, his mind wanted to correct. He refused to let the thought take root. They would get off the mountain before they ran out of food and water.

He would make sure of it.

Chapter Eleven

Whitney was pretty sure Jeremy had noticed that her limp had gotten worse. Had he been watching her walk to the cave? She'd tried to hide it, but when she tripped over a tree root, she nearly went down, twisting and wrenching her ankle further in her effort to stay upright. If she let herself think about it, her ankle felt like it was breaking in half. But she was trying not to focus on the pain. They had bigger things to worry about, like getting Sam—and themselves!—out of these woods and back home.

Plus, the truth was, she'd tripped because she'd been distracted. She'd thought she heard a woodpecker. Again. And when she'd looked up into the tree above her, where she could have sworn the knocking had come from, a root had reached up and grabbed her. Pulled her right down, as if it was saying, *Whitney! Get your head out of the clouds and pay attention to where you're going. There is no mystical woodpecker. There never was one. This is a moun-*

tain forest—there are going to be tons of woodpeck-ers. It means nothing.

The last had occurred to her as she was trying not to react to the ripping pain in her ankle. But she couldn't make herself believe it. Never was one? That was absolutely ridiculous. She knew what she had heard on her back door. She knew what she'd seen on the trail. Even if nobody else had seen it, she definitely had.

Okay, fine. Maybe the fact that nobody else had seen it wasn't exactly working in her favor.

Maybe she was losing it.

But she got the pack and brought it to Jeremy and Sam, regardless of ankles and woodpeckers.

Oh, man, she was so thirsty. She'd been aware of her dry throat before Sam had started guzzling that bottle of water Jeremy had given her. Hearing the girl's wet gulps only made Whitney's thirst seem so much worse.

Whitney licked her lips, to no avail, then crawled over to lean against a tree. She focused on loosening her shoestrings to keep from going mad at the sound of the crinkling of the bottle as Sam emptied it, the satisfied exhale when Sam was finally done drinking. Loosen the shoestrings, pull the shoe away from the ankle, rotate foot. *Ouch.*

Thirst was hardly her only problem. She was also hungry. And hot and tired and really, really scared. And lost. Finding Sam did nothing to change the fact that she was—they were—undeniably lost. She let her shoelace drop and fiddled with the walkie-talkie again, twisting the volume to make sure it was on full blast, hitting the call button several times, changing channels to see if maybe she could raise someone—anyone—even if it wasn't Rob. No such luck.

"What do we do now?" Sam asked, digging into a small bag of peanuts that she'd found at the bottom of the backpack. Whitney's stomach gurgled but she ignored it. She had way bigger problems than being a little hungry. And besides, she didn't like peanuts much, anyway. At least, that was what she was telling herself.

Jeremy glanced at Whitney before responding. She gave a tiny, almost imperceptible shrug.

Maybe it was just Whitney, but she could swear they'd been communicating without talking ever since they rescued Sam. How was that possible, when they barely knew each other? But she understood what his eyes were saying right now—he didn't know. He didn't know what they would do now, and he didn't know what to tell Sam, because he couldn't admit to her that he was without a plan, but he didn't want to lie to her, either. And, most of all, he hated both options. He wanted to have good news for her. He wanted to be positive and tell her she'd be sleeping in her own bed tonight. It tore him up that he wouldn't be able to.

She knew all of that from a glance.

Whitney had never had that happen with anyone before.

"We're going to get rescued," Whitney said brightly, scooting away from the tree so Sam was between them again. She patted Sam's back. "We're working on it."

Sam looked between Jeremy and Whitney, and Whitney could feel the hope building between the three of them. *See? This. This is what faith feels like*, Whitney wanted to tell Jeremy, even though she knew it was a waste of time. She averted her eyes, sad that he would never know that feeling.

Sad that she wasn't entirely sure she was feeling it herself. She was so thirsty. And so scared. Faith could sometimes be incredibly hard.

"How?" Sam asked. "Nobody knows where we are."

Whitney held up the walkie-talkie. "I keep checking. Eventually someone will be close enough to hear me."

"Or eventually we'll starve to death. Or be eaten by bears. Or fall into another hole." Sam looked doubtfully between Whitney and Jeremy. "I'm not a little kid anymore. I know this is bad."

Jeremy took a breath. "You're right," he said. "We're not in a great situation. But we're a long way from giving up. We can figure this out. We just have to have…" He faltered.

"Faith," Whitney supplied, and saw a flicker of recognition in his eyes. "And a good plan."

"Exactly," he said after the smallest beat. "Now, let's go at this rationally. Which way do we think the rest area is?"

They all pointed different directions, and even

though they knew it was only illustrating how lost they were, they giggled.

"Great," Sam said, rolling her eyes. "We just have to walk all over the whole entire mountain and we'll find it. It'll just be a hundred million miles. No big deal."

"No, wait, I think you're onto something," Jeremy said.

"What?" Whitney said. She couldn't even imagine making it a single mile at this point, much less traverse the entire mountain. It felt like they'd already done that. For all she knew, they had.

Jeremy held up his hand. "Just hear me out. Not the whole mountain, of course. But we could walk in concentric circles, a wider and wider radius, using the cave as our guide. We'll just always make sure we can see it. Maybe we'll find the path that way."

"Or maybe we'll fall in a hole," Sam said sullenly.

"We can't think like that," Whitney said. "We have to be positive."

"I'm positive that I fell into a hole," Sam grumbled.

"Which reminds me," Whitney said. "Follow my finger with just your eyes."

"Why?" Sam asked.

"I'm a nurse, and you've hit your head pretty hard. Just humor me." She held up a finger and moved it slowly, side to side in front of Sam's face, then, satisfied, took a good look at Sam's pupils. They were evenly dilated. She peppered Sam with questions: *Do you know why we're out here? Do you remember what the date is? What are the names of the other youth group leaders? Do you feel dizzy? Sleepy? Nauseous?*

Whitney could feel Jeremy watching the process intensely and felt proud that she could do this for Sam—and for him. She gave him a reassuring smile and nod, then stood, reaching down for one of Sam's hands. She would secretly assess the girl's balance once they got moving again.

"We're never going to get out of here," Sam whined. "Are we?"

Jeremy stood and grabbed Sam's other hand. "Come on, we got you out of the hole, didn't we? We'll get you off this mountain."

"Dad," Sam said, refusing to give up her sullenness. "I probably have a concussion, and we're going to starve to death in the forest."

"I'm pretty sure you don't have a concussion," Whitney said.

"And we're literally surrounded by things to eat," Jeremy added.

Sam's forehead crumpled in confusion. "Like what?"

Jeremy spread his arms out wide, and Whitney could sense a playfulness in him—a side she hadn't yet seen, but that seemed familiar to Sam. "Like that tree over there. You always said you wanted to be a vegetarian."

"No, I didn't," Sam said.

"Yummm, bark," he said. "Sounds tasty."

"Da-ad," Sam whined, but Whitney could see that she was breaking.

Whitney was taken back to time spent with her own mother, who loved to tease her and be silly to lighten the mood, even when times were terribly tough. Whitney remembered the days of adolescence when she would respond exactly the way that Sam was responding now. With complaints and whining, but a smile underneath. Only now she knew what the smile was about—someone cared enough to make her laugh. Someone was present enough to try to make her feel better.

Jeremy was that person for Sam. Not just the protector. The *everything*. No wonder he struggled with his faith. He never saw the hand that was holding *him* up—only his hand supporting Sam. When you were someone's everything, did it make it harder to see that you weren't alone? Whitney guessed that for Jeremy it might.

"She doesn't have to be a vegetarian," Whitney joined in. "I saw some spiders in the cave. Great protein."

Both Jeremy and Sam groaned disgustedly, but Sam allowed them to pull her to standing.

Chapter Twelve

They'd been walking for a long time. So long, Whitney and Sam had run out of camp songs, which they'd been singing as a way to keep their minds off of the uncomfortable things. Also to let Jeremy know that they were still behind him so he could stop looking backward every five steps to confirm it with his own eyes.

They'd seen a lot of squirrels. They'd found a vine that was great for swinging, and Whitney had sat to catch her breath while Sam took a swinging break. They'd stumbled across their tarp and rope from the night before, which felt like a small win. Whitney and Sam worked together to fold it into a square small enough to stuff back into Jeremy's pack.

But they never found the trail.

Whitney continued to try the walkie until she worried about the battery going dead. Even though nobody was responding to her call, the thought that she wouldn't be able to make the call anymore edged her with hopelessness that she dared not allow fully in.

They stopped to split a bottle of water, each taking tiny sips. Whitney tried not to notice that she wasn't sweating anymore, even though the air was warm and the walking and climbing was brisk. That was bad. She also tried to ignore that taking a tiny sip of water only ignited her desire for more. It was as if the water had never hit her tongue at all. Like it just… Evaporated.

That was worse.

She was a nurse. She knew very well the signs of dehydration.

"Everything looks the same," Sam said, turning in circles while Jeremy recapped the empty bottle and returned it to the pack with the others.

Whitney followed her. "Yeah, it really does," she said, tilting her face to the sky, which was blotted and mottled by trees. "It's sort of beautiful, though, don't you think?"

"Kind of. I like the way the sky looks through the leaves," Sam said. "It's really blue from down here where it's shady."

Jeremy treaded away from them. He'd produced a pair of binoculars and was studying the distance. *Look up, Jeremy*, Whitney thought. *Sam's right. It's gorgeous*.

"My mom's up there somewhere," Sam said, interrupting Whitney's thoughts.

Her words hit Whitney like a punch to the gut. Her already-dry throat tightened and she swallowed against it. After everything Jeremy had told her the night before, Whitney saw their loss differently. She thought maybe the best she could do for Sam was to let her know that she wasn't alone. "Mine, too," she answered.

Sam flicked a quick, inquisitive glance at Whitney, then turned back toward the sky. "I didn't know that."

"Yep," Whitney said. "Yesterday was my first birthday without her." Saying the words aloud left Whitney with a surreal feeling. Had it only been yesterday that she'd been trying to make the best of her day without her mom? She thought about the cupcakes in her pack, back at the rest area. Her jaw twinged, and she salivated with the memory of the creamy icing, the sugar crystals that had been sprinkled on top.

"I remember my first birthday without my mom," Sam said, very quietly. "My ninth birthday. I didn't want to have it. No party, no cake, nothing. I didn't even want to come out of my room." She grinned. "I mean, I still wanted presents."

Whitney chuckled. "Of course. Who doesn't?"

"So my dad canceled my party," Sam said. "He even told my grandma not to come, which made me feel a little bad because she was really upset about it and I heard her yelling at him over the phone."

"Did you have your party later, then?" Whitney asked, imaging a nine-year-old Sam, alone and sad on her birthday, crying for her mommy. It was almost more than Whitney could bear.

"Something better. On the day I was supposed to

have my party, my dad packed up our tent and sleeping bags and some hot dogs and cookies and stuff and we went to the lake, just the two of us. It was where we always spent my mom's birthday. She loved it there. So we went swimming until we were totally exhausted, and then we put up our tent, built a fire and roasted hot dogs for dinner. And then Dad sang 'Happy Birthday,' and we ate cookie s'mores. Have you ever had cookie s'mores?"

"No, I haven't," Whitney said. She glanced at Jeremy, who'd moved a few feet farther away and was standing on a fallen log, still gazing through his binoculars. Something inside of her trembled at the sight of him, and she realized she'd begun to see him in a different light. He'd gone from just the doubtful-looking overprotective and overprepared dad lurking around the perimeter of the church basement to a man who was there for the people he loved, no matter what. Who always had skin in the game, even if the skin was raw and scratched with every nerve exposed. Even if he'd lost the game before. *How do you do that?* Whitney wondered. *How do you make yourself vulnerable to love like that?*

"You should totally try them sometime," Sam continued. "It's like a regular s'more except between two soft chocolate chip cookies instead of two graham crackers. The chocolate chips get all melty, so it's extra chocolaty and gooey. They're so good. My mom made the best cookie s'mores. But my dad learned how to make them just like she did, because he knew they were my favorite. So we ate those, and then we went down to the beach and just sat in the sand and talked about how awesome my mom was."

Whitney could hear the buzzing of a helicopter off in the distance and hoped it was someone looking for them, but she couldn't express that hope aloud. This moment was too real for Sam. Too real for both of them.

"That sounds really great," Whitney said softly, imagining heartbroken Jeremy ignoring his own pain and making sure he celebrated Sam in the most healing way possible. How hard that must have been.

"It was the best." Sam wiped her eyes and turned so she was facing Whitney. "My dad cried a little, but don't tell him I told you that."

Whitney let out a breathless laugh, trying not to get teary-eyed herself. "I won't tell—"

Jeremy's sharp cry pulled them both out of their moment. They turned toward him. He was on the ground next to the log he'd been standing on, clutching his leg with both hands, his face screwed up in agony. Whitney had seen strange injuries, but never one from falling off a log. It didn't look high enough, but at this point, Whitney believed anything was possible.

"What happened?" Sam asked.

Whitney was already running toward him. Whatever had happened, it was bad. And not falling-off-a-log bad.

He was moaning, and big beads of sweat popped out on his beet-red forehead by the time Whitney had crossed the few feet to reach him.

"What happened? What is it?" she asked, immediately dropping to her knees by his side.

She was vaguely aware of Sam right behind her, crying, "Daddy?" over and over again, her voice filled with terrified tears.

"He's going to be okay," Whitney said, unsure if she was saying it to reassure Sam or Jeremy… Or herself. "What happened, Jeremy? Where are you hurt?"

"Snake," he finally said.

In an instant, Whitney popped back up onto her feet, her heart leaping into her throat. She was terrified of snakes. It hadn't even occurred to her before now that she might run across one out here. How silly of her not to even think about that. Of course there would be snakes in the forest. Where else would they be?

She heard Sam squeal and again went straight into reassurance mode. "It'll be okay."

"Came out from under that log," Jeremy said, using his head to gesture toward the hollow log that he'd been standing on. "I wasn't thinking. I didn't look. I may have stepped on it." This last was brought out on a wheeze of pain.

Whitney's eyes darted around the immediate area. She didn't see any snakes. If he'd stepped on it, he hadn't injured it very badly. Hopefully the snake retreated after administering its bite and was back in hiding, but without a snake to look at, they didn't know what kind of bite they were dealing with. A rat snake and a rattlesnake gave two very different bites. She could hear Sam's cries ratcheting up and knew she had to calm herself, to remain clearheaded.

"What…" She licked her lips with her dry tongue. "What kind? Did you see what kind of snake?"

"I think…copperhead. No, I'm pretty sure. Copperhead." He'd let go of his leg and was now doubled over with both arms clutching his stomach. "I'm going to be sick."

"Okay," Whitney said, more to herself than anyone else. "Okay, okay, okay. Think, Whitney, think. Okay, first, take care of Sam." She turned to the little girl, who was near hysterics watching her father writhe on the ground. She placed her hands on both of Sam's cheeks, steadying her and forcing her to look right into her eyes. They'd studied local snakes in their mountaineering training. There were several venomous snakes that could be out here, and Whitney was pretty sure copperhead was the least potent. Or was that the cottonmouth? No, she was pretty sure the copperhead was the better bite to get, if you were going to get a bite. Definitely better. "Honey, I need you to calm down. Remember our training." She looked around. "Copperheads aren't deadly. He's going to be fine. But he's in a lot of pain and I need to help him, so you're going to have to take a few breaths. See that rock over there?" She pointed to a large, flat boulder nearby. She would feel much better if she knew that Sam was free of snakebite possibility. "Go over and stand on that rock and I'm going to help your dad, okay? Calmly."

Sam nodded, her head moving frantically, her eyes round and wide as quarters.

"It's going to be okay," Whitney said again, looking deep into the child's eyes. *I won't let you down,* she wanted to say, realizing that this was something Jeremy would promise. She could understand now how easy it was to make that sort of vow. How easy it was to put that skin in the game, when the game was just right.

Sam nodded again, then slowly moved toward the rock, where she climbed up and squatted, locking her arms around her knees, her eyes glued to her father. Whitney went back to him.

"Okay," she said. "Let's see the bite."

"Leg," he croaked. He was waxy and pale, and his skin felt clammy as Whitney pulled the cuff of his pant leg up to reveal the bite. There were two faintly bleeding holes, and already the skin of his lower leg was turning blue and swelling.

"Are you dizzy?" she asked.

He nodded miserably. "Weak."

"Let me get you some water."

"No, no," he said. "Save it."

She turned his body, so she could get into the backpack still strapped to him, and pulled out an unopened water. "No, you need it."

"Sam."

She unscrewed the top and lifted his head with the crook of her arm, then dribbled a tiny bit into his mouth. "Sam needs you," she said. "She needs to see you drink this water. Come on."

He opened his mouth slightly but choked when she poured a little too hastily. His coughing turned back to moaning, and he rolled away from her. "You're right," he panted. "She needs me. I can't... I can't..."

"Listen to me," Whitney said, capping the water and setting it aside. She touched his cheeks with both palms, just as she'd done with his daughter moments before. While Sam's had felt hot and wet with tears, his were cold and damp in a sickly way. "Listen. You're not going to die, so you're not even going to talk about it. Sam does not need to hear you say that kind of thing. Concentrate. We learned about these bites in training, remember? You're going to feel horrible, and your leg is going to swell like crazy and you may lose some tissue. But the calmer you stay, the slower the venom circulates through your system. So...stay...calm."

It was all coming back to her now. That sucking the venom out of a snakebite was a myth. That once it was in, it was in. That a copperhead's venom wouldn't likely kill anyone larger than a raccoon. That the snake was more scared of them than they were of it and had definitely fled to safety after striking. Nausea, vomiting, weakness, chills, terrible pain. Staying calm was key.

"Look at me, Jeremy," she said, turning his face toward hers, deliberately dropping her voice into what she thought of as her Soothing Nurse Voice. "Look." His eyes found hers. "You're going to be all right. Let's breathe together. Ready?"

His whole body shivered as he followed her lead,

but his eyes never left hers. They breathed in and out together.

"Think about…think about the lake. Sitting on the beach. Eating cookie s'mores. Soft chocolate chips, melty chocolate, perfectly toasted marshmallow. Yes, you've got it. Breathe in and out, slowly, slowly. Good."

Eventually, his eyes squeezed shut again, but he was much calmer. Whitney let him have a moment, then tried the water again.

"Can you drink?"

He shook his head. "Nauseous."

She put the water down. "Can you sit? For Sam?"

He nodded. Whitney wrapped her arm around his neck and helped him as he painfully pulled to a seated position. She didn't have any real reason behind it, but an instinct told her that getting his heart elevated above the venom was a good thing. He leaned forward, his head hanging as he gasped for breath. Whitney could feel him holding back, his whole frame shuddering with every exhale.

She chanced a look over her shoulder, where Sam still crouched on the rock, tears streaming down her face. She, too, looked calmer.

"He's okay," Whitney called. "He'll be okay."

But in the back of her mind she couldn't help wondering if he would be okay. If they could get him out of the woods and to help quickly, then yes, definitely. But lost in the woods, nothing to combat the venom, little food and water, no real shelter, no sort of antiseptic… Did that change the odds? It certainly couldn't improve them.

That only makes taking care of him more important. But she'd never had to nurse someone back to health under circumstances such as these. Once again, she leaned on the crutch she'd been leaning on literally since the day she was born. *Mom? If you're there, I could use some help here. I'm kind of out of my element.*

But Whitney knew one thing—her mom never thought she needed a crutch at all. She always trusted her to do the right thing. Always had the fullest faith in her. Always believed that she could accomplish whatever she set her mind to. It had given Whitney confidence when she most needed it. She would need to rely on that confidence now.

"Okay," she said. "I'm going to pour a little water over the wound. I know we don't want to waste water, but we also need to try to make sure it's as clean as possible."

She twisted the cap off the water bottle as she talked and was pouring the water before her sentence was finished, to give Jeremy as little chance as possible to argue. Not that he did. The heat of the poison made his skin angry and hot. He sucked in a breath through his teeth as she dribbled water over the snakebite, but then just clenched his fists in his lap. She patted his back lightly, feeling sweat soak through his shirt and dampen the palm of her hand.

Wordlessly, she helped him slide the pack off his shoulders and set it aside. She pulled the tarp out and unfolded it into a square big enough for a pillow, then helped ease him back down.

"You rest while I figure out what to do next," she said.

He looked as if he wanted to argue, but simply nodded, his eyes closed, his energy spent.

She stared at him for a few long moments. His waxy complexion and closed eyes were frightening, but he still looked strong in some way that she couldn't quite wrap her mind around. She knew that inside he was thinking of Sam. She knew that he didn't want to leave Sam behind.

Whitney couldn't help it—tears began to fall. She needed to be strong, but suddenly she felt so overwhelmed. Not just by their situation, but by loss in general. Her own loss, Jeremy's loss and what if Sam now lost him too? Her breath hitched at the thought of Sam, who had traversed the biggest grief of her life, possibly having to traverse it again three years later. She wanted to lie down and close her eyes, too. Be done with this. Be done with pain. Be done with loving and losing. Done with loving at all.

"What?" she heard behind her. "What's wrong? Is something wrong? Why are you crying?" Each question was asked in a higher pitch than the one before— a crescendo of the unimaginable coming to fruition. The last came out nearly a shriek, sending Whitney into instant motion, whether she wanted to give up or not. "Is he dying?"

"No, no-no-no," Whitney said, rushing to Sam. She wrapped the girl in her arms and rocked with her, shushing her even while their tears intermingled. They sat that way for what seemed like a long time, until the tears stopped and the shushing was the only thing to be heard, the rocking the only movement.

Eventually, Whitney allowed herself to look up, her eyes immediately going to Jeremy, who twitched and winced every so often but otherwise looked peaceful. She was going to have to plan their next action without his input.

A movement caught Whitney's attention. A fluttering blur of black, white and red. She watched as a bird flew directly through her line of sight and then landed on a branch just above Jeremy. It tilted its head this way and that, regarding Whitney.

Her mouth dropped open. She blinked a few times. Surely she was imagining this. But the bird issued a loud call—almost sounding to Whitney like a small dog barking—causing Sam to look up, too.

"What's that?" Sam asked. Whitney struggled not to cheer that someone else was seeing and hearing this. It wasn't her imagination. She wasn't going crazy.

But that only begged the question—why was this woodpecker following her? Whitney didn't know for sure, but she definitely had a theory that whatever it was there for, it was for her benefit.

"It's a woodpecker," she said. "Isn't he beautiful?"

"It's loud," Sam said. "It's not going to attack Dad, is it?"

Whitney shook her head, her face softening into a grin. "No. I really don't think so."

Sam wiped her nose on the back of her hand and turned her attention to her dad, the woodpecker quickly forgotten. "Is he going to be okay?"

Whitney hugged her tighter. "I think he will. But he's in a lot of pain. And…" *And now we really need to be rescued sooner rather than later*, she didn't finish. "And he needs us to be strong and positive for him, okay?"

Sam nodded.

"So let's see what's in this pack," Whitney said, sliding off the rock and grabbing Jeremy's backpack. Sam followed her, scanning the ground worriedly.

"The snake…" she said in a small voice.

"It's gone," Whitney said. "We can't think about the snake right now. Help me inventory this. Do you think he would mind?"

Sam shook her head.

"Did you bring any supplies with you?" Whitney asked, realizing only now that Sam was not carrying a backpack. Maybe it was at the bottom of the crevasse. If it had worthwhile supplies in it, they could go back and try to retrieve it.

Sam shook her head. "Lily and I combined bags. She was wearing it. But there wasn't much in it anyway, because Mr. Rob told us not to bring a bunch of stuff with us. There were KitKats in it, though. I wish I had one right now."

"Me, too," Whitney said, although the adrenaline and worry had caused her stomach to no longer clench with hunger. She recognized this as an opportunity to keep Sam calm. "And a great, big cheeseburger to go with it."

"And macaroni and cheese," Sam said.

"Oh, yes. And a huge Coke. A giant bucket of Coke."

They took the bag to the rock and began laying items on top of it. The last full water bottle, the rope that had still been stuck to the tarp when they found it, the survival blanket, some bandages and ointment, a cell phone, a wallet, a knife, a lighter, a handful of granola bars and a plastic baggie filled with trail mix. Whitney set aside the bandages and ointment and tossed everything else back in the bag. Sam snatched the trail mix and ripped into it.

"Go easy," Whitney said. "You'll make yourself thirsty, and we don't have much water left."

"I don't care," Sam said around a mouthful. "I'm so hungry."

"Well, while you do that, let me see that bump on your head." Whitney pushed back Sam's hair and was shocked at the huge, bruised lump hidden in her hair. It hadn't gone down any. And the cut in the center looked like it could start bleeding again at any moment. It really could have used a few stitches.

Whitney squeezed some ointment onto her finger and gently dabbed it against the cut. Sam recoiled, but then went back to her trail mix and let Whitney finish.

"You know, you're pretty tough."

Sam didn't respond.

"I don't know if I'd be as tough as you if I'd hit my head like that."

Sam swallowed. Half the bag was already gone. The scent of nuts and chocolate were making Whitney woozy with craving. "When you were walking back from the cave, Dad said you were tough, because you sprained your ankle, or maybe even broke it, but you don't complain at all. He said he admires you."

Whitney paused, taken aback. "He said that?"

Sam nodded. "Yeah. He said he wouldn't have been able to find me or get me out of that dumb hole if it wasn't for you."

Whitney blinked. She'd felt like a burden this entire time. She was sure he was thinking he'd have found Sam so much faster if it wasn't for her following him, or falling, or hurting herself. She never would have guessed that he'd actually needed her.

"Well, that was very kind of him to say," she said. "I think your dad is pretty admirable, too. And very tough himself. And that's how I know no silly snakebite is going to take him down. I guess that means we're all pretty tough, huh?"

Sam shrugged, focused on the food. "Yeah."

Whitney unpackaged a bandage and spread it over the cut on Sam's forehead. It didn't cover the whole thing, so she unpackaged another, and then a third.

"There you go," she said, and leaned over and lightly kissed the spot on Sam's head before even thinking about what she was doing. Sam paused, only briefly, and went back to the trail mix without a word.

Whitney carried the ointment and bandages to Jeremy, who still lay sprawled out on the ground. She glanced to the branch above him again, but the woodpecker was gone. A cloud passed over the sun, creating a hazy darkness. She thought she heard a low rumble. Surely not rain again. Another storm like last night? How would she get them to cover?

"Hey," she said. "I'm going to put some stuff on that bite, okay?"

Jeremy didn't answer but nodded.

She leaned over his leg with the pant leg still pulled up. The skin had darkened and the swelling had gotten worse. His ankle looked puffier than hers. Gently, gently, she dabbed some ointment onto the bite and then stretched a bandage over it. Again, he sucked in a breath through his teeth, but when she jumped back, he reached down and patted her elbow softly.

"Thank you," he croaked. Butterflies hopped around in Whitney's stomach, unbidden. She nearly gasped with surprise. She was beginning to feel something for him. Something real and wonderful and terrifying. She wanted to ignore it but found that she couldn't. She had a sinking suspicion that if she opened herself up to Jeremy, her heart could be in real danger.

Still. She reached over and placed her hand on top of his. "You're welcome. More water?"

He shook his head, but as if to answer her question, the sky darkened further and a much louder rumble shook them. All three studied the sky.

"We need to get back to the cave," Jeremy said, but still his voice was barely more than a whisper.

Whitney didn't see how that would be at all possible. "I could set up the tarp. I could do it right here over you, so you wouldn't have to move."

He shook his head and struggled to an upright position. "I can get there."

"I don't know…" she said, but another clap of thunder ended the argument.

Just like the day before, they could hear the rain splattering against the leaves before they could see or feel it below. Whitney thought she would be happy if she never had to hear the sound of raindrops hitting leaves ever again.

She sprang into action, throwing the tarp and first aid kit back into the pack and slinging its straps over her arms.

"Come on, Sam," she said. "Help me get your dad up. We have to get back to the cave."

Chapter Thirteen

Their trek to the safety of the cave was very slow. Jeremy's weight was overwhelming, and even though Sam took the backpack to lighten Whitney's load, the rain and sweat had made their skin slick, forcing Whitney to cling to Jeremy with everything she had to keep him from falling away. He leaned heavily on her, stopping and clutching his stomach every few feet, swaying from dizziness and nausea. Twice he lurched away to be sick, knocking Whitney to her knees with the sudden motion. Her muscles ached and her ankle screamed, and the cave seemed an impossible distance away.

The mountain seemed so steep—even steeper than it had seemed the night before when she was the one who needed help. Whitney was well aware the last several feet leading to the cave entrance were rocky and unstable. She wasn't sure how she was going to traverse the distance herself, much less get him up there.

She was so tired.

Empty. And tired.

But Jeremy hadn't stopped, and he certainly hadn't given up on her, so Whitney refused to give up or stop on him. She tried to tell herself it was a matter of repayment, but deep inside she knew it was something more. She understood him now. And with that understanding came an even stronger desire to get through this with him.

Whitney and Jeremy were both scratched and bruised from being unable to shield themselves from the slap of limbs and grasp of weeds. Whitney's palms were scraped from falling on them. And both of them were limping greatly. They must have made for an unsightly pair.

The temperature had dropped and the wind had picked up, rushing down the mountain in gusts and gales, driving the raindrops into their eyes, their ears, their skin. Sam's entire body quaked and shivered as she caught up with Whitney. Her knees looked ready to buckle.

No, not an unsightly *pair*. They made for an unsightly *trio*.

Whitney paused at the bottom of the final incline to the cave entrance. "Can you take the bag up?" Sam nodded and scrambled up the rocks, her shoes only slipping once or twice as they knocked gravel loose. She crawled into the tiny opening, then turned around and poked her head out. "Good!" Whitney called.

She chewed her lip, assessing the situation. How was she going to get Jeremy up this last hill? Sam had only slipped a couple of times, but if Jeremy started to slide, Whitney wouldn't physically be able to stop him, would she? They would both tumble down, and they couldn't afford any more injuries.

"Jeremy?" she asked, talking loudly, even though she was right in his ear. The noise of the storm was picking up. He lifted his head. "We've got to work together. It's just…it's just a few feet. I need you to use all of your strength, okay? Everything you've got. For Sam."

She said the last, knowing that if anything would muster Jeremy's strength, it would be the thought of his daughter. It worked. He nodded, and she felt some of his weight lift off of her as he straightened to full standing.

"We'll go together, okay?" Whitney said, approaching the rocky incline.

Again, Jeremy nodded, and he lurched to her side, grunting as he put weight on his snakebit leg. It sounded like rage—a sound that heartened Whitney. Rage meant effort.

They crept up the hill together, one step at a time, and when they reached the cave opening, Whitney crawled inside first before stretching to give Jeremy a hand. He fell to his knees and then stopped. At first, his weight seemed to be more intent on pulling her out of the cave and back down the mountain. Whitney thought about the first time she, as a new nursing student, had to lift a patient to change bedding. At five foot four inches tall and one hundred and ten pounds, she had been sure she would never be able to be a nurse with heavy lifting as a requirement. But the patient, easily one hundred pounds heavier than her, looked at her with such gratitude, she'd somehow found the strength within herself to get the job done. It wasn't even as hard as she thought it would be. And years of nursing had proven to her that she had far more physical strength than she ever thought she did.

She channeled that first moment now, wrapped her arms around his waist, and gave a yank harder than she'd ever pulled anything in her life, letting out a frustrated cry as she did so. Soon she was backing into the cave, heaving him along with her. Whitney couldn't tell if it was sweat or rain that poured from his face, but guessed it was a pretty even mixture of both. She laid him back on the cave floor, then scooted out of the way to give him plenty of room.

Sam lay on the floor next to him, her arm wrapped around his chest protectively. Whitney leaned back against the wall and let her muscles rest. It was hard to believe all three of them fit inside the cave—last night the two of them seemed to fill it completely— but somehow they all did.

Had the cave been bigger than she'd originally thought, or had her perception of being this close to Jeremy changed? She wasn't sure.

The rain went on and on, and Jeremy's gasps turned into even snores. He was sleeping, and Whitney hoped that meant the worst of his pain had passed. She clasped her hands together and bowed her head. "God, please let him rest in comfort," she whispered. While it was certainly not unheard of for her to say a quick prayer over a patient, it was against everything she'd been trained to do to let a patient wear themselves out with pain, but she had no choice. She couldn't comfort him herself, but she could ask God to, and hope that He heard her plea.

A flash of lightning captured her attention. Suddenly, she had an idea. She couldn't believe she hadn't thought of it before now. She grabbed the backpack and opened it, then quickly pulled out the tarp, the rope and the knife.

The ointment and bandages fell out onto the floor as she shook out the tarp. She picked them up and unzipped a front pocket to store them in there, but her hand fell on something square and flat instead. She pulled it out.

It was a sodden and curling photo. A blonde woman with a huge smile, holding a bundle of blankets in her arms. Next to her stood a younger Jeremy, looking worry free and profoundly happy as he gazed down at the bundle.

"That's my mom," Sam whispered, making Whitney jump. Sam was still lying next to her father but had propped her head up on one elbow and was gazing at Whitney. She'd stopped shivering, though her hair still fell in limp, wet strings.

"I'm sorry. I wasn't—"

"It's okay. He always has that picture with him. It's his favorite. It was the day they brought me home from the hospital. He says my mom was the most beautiful woman in the world that day. But I was a close number two." She lifted her hand, and Whitney placed the photograph in it.

"It's wet," Whitney said. "From the rain."

Sam frowned, but laid the photo down on the ground and smoothed it over with her fingers. "It'll dry out. You can still see her smile. That's my favorite part about it."

"Mine, too," Whitney said. "She was very beautiful."

"Was your mom beautiful, too?" Sam asked.

Whitney felt a stab in her chest. Nobody had ever asked her that before, so she'd never really thought about it. Her mom had brilliant green eyes and an upturned mouth that made her always look like she was smiling. She was round and soft and always had the perfect handbag to go with every occasion. She taught Whitney how to French braid and how to highlight cheekbones with blush and how much to tip a hairstylist. Her skin was fair and smooth and soft like cotton sheets, and when Whitney was young, she liked to hold her mom's hand and study the veins on the backs of them that made them look so mature and exotic. "Yes," she said. "My mother was very beautiful, too. In a lot of different ways."

"Sometimes I think my mom is an angel in a shiny white dress. She would really like that," Sam said. "She liked shiny things."

"She'd be a lovely angel," Whitney agreed. "And if she liked shiny things, I'm sure she's got all the shiny things she could ever imagine right now."

Sam was quiet for a long time, staring at and occasionally dabbing the water off of the picture of her mother.

Whitney didn't want to interrupt this time Sam had with her mom, plus she wanted to execute her idea before the rain stopped, so she cut the two pieces of rope into four shorter pieces and knotted them through holes in the tarp. Once the knots were secure, Whitney grabbed the tarp and the knife and climbed out of the cave, back into the rain, which felt like cold gravel pelting her skin.

She scooted down most of the hill on her behind, wanting to save her ankle and prevent a slip and fall. She held tight to the tarp so the wind wouldn't steal it from her again. When she reached the place where the mountain's slope was flatter, she half trotted into the trees, found four that were in a close bunch and tied four corners of the tarp to their branches, leaving slack so that the tarp would droop in the middle. Immediately, it began to fill with a small puddle of rain. Whitney dropped to her knees and pressed on one edge of the tarp, tipping it so the puddle slid toward her. She drank two big sips of water, her mouth and throat screaming with relief. She let the tarp droop again and sat beneath it, letting the tap of the rain lull her, and then crawled out and repeated the procedure. The water tasted green and a little gritty from falling through the canopy of leaves, but she didn't care. It was water. And if the rain kept up, they would have plenty to refill their empty bottles in the morning. She hadn't questioned why Jeremy had saved the empties, but now she was so glad that he had.

Satisfied, she headed back to the cave, rushing up the incline with much more ease than she had before. *Amazing what a little hydration can do*, she thought. She was almost giddy at the thought of filling their bottles soon. When she got inside, just for added measure, she found two of their empty bottles and set them upright just inside the mouth of the cave. The rain barely hit the edge, and it filled much more slowly, but it was something. She took out their last bottle and handed it to Sam.

"You can have some," she said. "And so can your dad."

Sam took the bottle and sat up. She peered out at the tarp that Whitney had set up. The puddle in the middle had grown already. Surprisingly, she didn't ask any questions. She seemed to understand Whitney's plan by looking.

Finally, Sam took a drink, and then another. "Did anyone sing to you?"

"Huh?"

"'Happy Birthday.' Did anyone sing it for you yesterday?"

Whitney shook her head. "We were going to do that when we got to the peak."

Sam took another drink, then set the bottle on the ground next to Jeremy's head. "I want to sing to you."

Whitney opened her mouth to protest but found that she couldn't do it. She was too touched by the sentiment. "You want to—"

But she didn't get the full sentence out before Sam

started singing. *"Happy birthday to you, happy birthday to you..."*

Whitney let out a choked little laugh, and then her breath caught as she realized Sam's song had taken on a little echo. Only it wasn't an echo at all. It was Jeremy, his voice small and tired, singing along with her.

"...happy birthday to you!" Sam finished strong and joined Whitney in applause at the end of her song. "Sorry we don't have a cake for you," she said. "Want a granola bar instead?" She held up one of the coveted last few granola bars.

Whitney smiled and took the bar, unwrapped it and broke off a piece. "Only if you share it with me." She broke off another piece. "Both of you." Jeremy reached up to take the food, but never took a bite before falling asleep again, holding the food in his hand.

It could hardly be called a dinner, but the granola bar had seemed to settle both Whitney's and Sam's stomachs. It was chilly outside, and they were wet, and as night fell, they were only going to get colder. But the survival blanket had had a day to dry, and Whitney thought they could all three fit under it if they squeezed close. She pulled it out of the backpack and spread it out and, soon after, Sam curled up under it with her head on the backpack and fell asleep, too.

But Whitney couldn't sleep. She couldn't stop hearing Sam's sweet voice singing to her. Couldn't stop marveling over the fact that Jeremy had joined in, even though he was so sick. She thought about the woodpecker they'd seen earlier, after he'd been bitten, just before the storm hit. Was there a reason it had shown itself to both Whitney and Sam this time, instead of just Whitney alone? It seemed doubtful, but Whitney couldn't help wondering if there was something to it.

She glanced back at Sam, who lay so still and satisfied with that photo, and Whitney couldn't help wondering if anyone would ever hold a photo of her like that. Would she ever provide such a sense of love for someone that the mere act of her existence made them feel safe?

Did she want to?

I want to sing to you...

For the first time ever, she thought maybe, just maybe she did. She was rattled by this realization.

And by the realization that she no longer wanted to survive this just for herself.

She pulled out her cell phone and sent a text to Cindy and Rob, even though she still didn't have any coverage. It was worth a shot.

We found Sam. We're very lost. If you see a cave where two of the mountains meet, we are in it. We are also close to a crevasse. And somewhat close to a big cliff. Look for a blue tarp strung between four trees collecting water. We have injuries.

Please find us.

Chapter Fourteen

When Jeremy woke the first time, Whitney was sitting in the cave opening, staring out into the rain. He made no movement, no sound. Just watched her as she checked the bottles she'd set in the cave opening. They were about a quarter full. She pushed them out a little farther, but not so far that the wind could send them tumbling down the hill.

She was smart. He knew that going in, but the water thing... He wasn't sure if he would have thought of it.

Lightning had begun flashing high up in the sky now. Rapid, noiseless flashes that seared her silhouette into his eyes so that when he closed them, she was what he saw. He didn't mind. In fact, he took it as his chance to really study her, even if it was only the afterimage of her. There was something about Whitney that was comforting and familiar. The phrase that kept coming to mind as her image faded behind his eyelids: *coming home again*. He dozed, puzzling over what this could mean for him.

It was sniffling that woke him the second time. She'd moved away from the ledge and now sat with her back against the cave wall. She was staring at Sam, softly weeping. He watched as she reached over and smoothed Sam's hair off of her face, a gesture so tender, it moved him to speak.

"Hey," he whispered. She jerked her hand away from Sam, as if she'd been caught doing something she wasn't supposed to. He held back a chuckle, felt his lips crack with the attempt to smile.

"Hey," she whispered, quickly wiping the tears from her cheeks and offering him a wobbly smile in return. "How are you?"

"Better, I think," he said. "Do we have water?"

She moved quickly, scuffling around the edge of the cave in a squat, and had a bottle pressed up to his mouth before, it seemed to him, he'd even gotten the full question out.

"Sit up a little?" she whispered as she slid her hand behind his neck. It was cool and comforting. Goose bumps rose on his arms as he let her guide him upward for a sip and then a gulp and then another. He would have liked to believe it was the chill from the wind and the rain that brought about the goose bumps, but he suspected it was something more. Something... Whitney.

He pulled away from the bottle, not wanting to drink it all and fearing that he just might.

"It's okay," she said, seemingly reading his mind.

"I've got the tarp collecting rain. Last I looked, it had more than enough to refill our bottles. Maybe a couple times. Tastes a little like trees, but it's not bad." She tipped the bottle and he drank more, unaware how thirsty he was until the bottle had gone dry and he still wanted more. She laid his head back down on the rocky ground. "You feel sick?"

He shook his head.

"How's your leg?"

"Numb," he said, knowing that, while it was a blessing to be out from under the radiating pain of the bite, it was probably not good to have gone completely without feeling. The crease that feathered its way between her eyebrows verified that for him. Was numbness a sign of tissue dying? He didn't want to ask. He would save that question for the doctor once he got off this mountain. "I'm sure I'll be able to hike by morning." It was a lie, and they both knew it. He was sure of no such thing.

She patted his shoulder. "You should just concentrate on getting some rest tonight. We'll worry about tomorrow, tomorrow."

"Right. Tomorrow we'll go home." He meant to sound optimistic—confident, even—but understood that his words rang sarcastic. He wanted to take them back. Instead, he reached for her hand. "I mean that."

"I know. From your lips to God's ears."

"From my lips to Rob's ears," he joked, but realized that again he sounded sarcastic and regretted his decision. Fortunately, Whitney was polite enough or forgiving enough to chuckle. He let his eyes slip closed again. Her afterimage was gone, regretfully.

"Thank you for the song earlier."

He reopened his eyes. Her smile had been replaced by a much more pensive look. She was fiddling with her fingers. Tears had sprung up again and slowly slid their way down her cheeks.

"Hey, you okay?" he asked.

She nodded, then changed course and shook her head instead. "I'm so worried that we won't get found."

He opened his mouth to reassure her, but found that he couldn't. This woman deserved the truth, not reassurances. And nothing he was saying was coming out right anyway. "I know," he said. "Me, too."

"I'm not even that worried about me," she said. "There's not…there's nobody out there waiting for me, really."

"That can't be true," he said.

She shrugged. "Well… Friends, I guess. A few cousins and aunts and uncles, maybe. Coworkers. Cindy. I've… I guess I've kind of kept myself closed off. People would be sad, and it would definitely be on the news, but it wouldn't really be that long before nobody even remembered me, much less missed me."

"I would miss you," he blurted, without thinking about how he sounded. What was wrong with him? Why couldn't he get a word out that sounded the way he meant it right now? Why couldn't he speak without second-guessing himself? Maybe the venom had messed with his brain. Maybe the poison was making

him unable to put words together without sounding…
Sounding what, exactly? Weak? Silly?

In love?

He took a breath, chased that last thought away.
Of course he wasn't in love. He'd only just gotten to
know her, and besides, he had one love in his life:
Laura. And she was gone and he didn't intend to re-
place her. Ever. He had Sam to worry about.

"It's Sam I worry about," Whitney said, echoing
his very thought. He was starting to wonder if this
was even reality. Maybe it was a dream. She couldn't
be *that* in tune with him in real life, could she? "She's
already lost so much. What if…" She trailed off, but
Jeremy knew what she was thinking. What if Sam lost
him, too? He'd wondered the same thing many times
since this journey began. There was no good answer.

She would have his mother and father, certainly.
They loved her and they were really good grandpar-
ents. But they were older. Quite a bit older. It would
only set her up to lose at an impossibly young age
again. How many times could a young person expe-
rience loss and not end up… Changed?

And Laura's parents, while younger, lived in Se-
attle. They wouldn't argue about taking in Sam, but
they wouldn't interrupt their own lives too much to
accommodate her. They would find people to watch
her. She would lose again. Her friends, her surroundings. Her comfort. She would be something that Jeremy had worked his hardest to prevent: lonely.

And then there was Whitney. She'd stuck by him
throughout all of this. She was sticking by Sam. And,

well, he was lying to himself when he pretended he wasn't interested in seeing what their friendship could turn into outside of this forest. The truth was, he wanted more. He wanted to know who this woman was when she wasn't fighting for her life, or his life, or Sam's. He wanted to know what kind of perfume she wore and where she went to school and who was her favorite band. He wanted to hear about her day at work and listen to her clanking around the kitchen while making birthday cupcakes for herself. He wanted to be delighted by her. He wanted to watch her put together jigsaw puzzles on the living room floor with Sam—something he'd never thought he would want to see anyone but Laura do.

It was all more than he could take. He had to get better and he had to get them out of this forest. Non-negotiable. He had to be there for his daughter. For life. He'd promised her. He'd promised Laura. But most of all, he'd promised himself.

"I would take care of her," Whitney said. Even she looked surprised by her decision. "If something happens…to you. I would make sure she's okay. I think she would trust me."

"Nothing's going to happen to me," he said.

"I know. I'm just saying. If we got out of here and you didn't…you could count on me."

He knew this was true. He couldn't explain it in words; it was more of a feeling. A feeling of someone who was put into your path for a reason. It was something he'd never thought he'd feel again. Something he'd convinced himself he'd only imagined feeling the first time.

Because if there was anything he learned from Laura's death, it was that when someone is gone, they're gone. Poof. Out of your path. They may leave footprints behind, but they were not waiting for you somewhere down the road. They were not there for you at all anymore.

But Whitney made him doubt that. Made him even wonder, despite himself, if Laura had put Whitney in his path herself.

Maybe that was what happened. Maybe when someone stepped off your path, they were simply making room for others who belonged there.

Or maybe he was still delirious from the snakebite. That made so much more sense to him than any of this.

"And if I…" Whitney paused, wiped her nose with the back of her hand. "If I don't make it out of here… I just wanted to tell you I think you're a really great dad. And I'm sorry."

"Sorry? For what?"

"For getting you into this. For planning the hike to begin with, and then making you feel silly for having so much packed into your backpack. For hurting my ankle and slowing you down from finding her faster. For leaving my backpack behind. For all of it." Her hands drifted to her ankle and rested lightly there, as if she were trying to hide it from him.

He struggled to a seated position, wincing against a lightning bolt of pain followed by a swimmy wooziness, but careful to be quiet so he didn't wake Sam. "You have nothing to be sorry about. I'm so thankful you were here. I—we—needed you. I didn't know it at first, but I know it now." He reached over and placed his hand on top of hers, which was warm and dry, a slight tremor rocking it. "You couldn't have foreseen this. Nobody could have."

"You did," she said.

He sighed. "I see risk everywhere I go. It's what I do. People die walking into grocery stores and sitting at their kitchen tables. And working in their own restaurants. Life is risk. I don't like it, but that doesn't change the fact. Laura was safe. I did everything I could to keep her safe. And she still died."

Something was building inside of him. Something he'd felt only peripherally. Something he'd kept himself from feeling fully. But Whitney was looking at him with such sympathy. Her hand was so warm under his, and he… Well, he trusted her. And that was never supposed to happen again. And the injustice that had been filling him for three years was spilling over as he warred with himself over what was and what should have been. He closed his eyes, willing himself not to shout or cry or… He didn't even know what. But when he opened them again and saw Whitney's empathetic eyes mine into his and felt her soft, patient exhalations filling the cave around them, what he'd been holding back since the day of Laura's funeral finally spilled over.

"We were supposed to have a life together. A whole life. We were supposed to watch Sam grow up and graduate and go to college and get married. We were supposed to spoil grandchildren together. It's not fair or right or easy or decent. It just is. And you have to accept it no matter how much you don't want to. And you have to watch your child get the biggest lesson in unfairness that she'll ever get. And you have to sit by and let it happen and hope that she can put the pieces back together in some way that makes some sort of sense." He let out an anguished breath that was somewhere between a sigh and a cry. "I still have to be all the things Laura wanted. I just have to be them by myself now. And I'm angry that she's not here with me. I'm angry that she didn't lock the back door that night. I'm angry that she didn't run away or call the police or do anything to save herself. And I feel guilty for feeling all this anger. But that still doesn't make me not feel it." It had to be the venom coursing through his blood. Had to be. He'd felt these things for three years, but had never allowed himself to really dwell on them, much less express them. Now he was by turns a fountain of cosmic rage and a hopeless puppy dog romantic. It was exhausting.

Whitney was quiet for a moment. "Have you told her these things?"

"No, of course not. She's dead. I can't talk to her."

"But you can," she said. "It's not really prayer. It's a conversation. She's not physically here, but she can hear you. I know it."

"Like I told you, I believed, and this is where it got me. I just don't know if I'll ever be able to believe again. I don't even have time for it. There are things to be done here. With the live people who are left behind. That would be me."

They were quiet again. Jeremy was shocked at how much he'd piled onto Whitney. She'd started this conversation by offering to be there for his daughter, and he'd responded by telling her how unfair the world was and then insulting her beliefs. He didn't mean to be unkind. And he felt guilty about it.

"I'm sorry," he said. "It's just how I feel."

"It's okay," she said, but he could feel her pulling away from him. Could feel her disappointment in him. He could feel his own disappointment in himself.

"I'm not telling you what to believe," she said. "But I saw a woodpecker." He was confused by this sudden and extreme shift in conversation that only made this seem more like a fever dream. "On the branch right above you, after you got bitten. Sam saw it, too."

"There are lots of birds in the woods."

"But none of them sat on a branch and stared at us just as a rainstorm was coming in," she said. "And it's the third one I've seen in two days. Or the third time I've seen this one. I don't know."

"That's…strange," he said. He had no idea what she was getting at, although he supposed that when it came to seeing things you want to see, woodpeckers could be on the list, too.

"It's very strange," she said. "And it's also the reason I talk to my mom. Because there are so many very strange things that happen that nobody can explain. Those things are divine. Maybe we're not meant to understand every woodpecker that flies into our lives."

"There's no woodpecker in my life," he said.

"But maybe there is," she said, "and you're too busy saying that it doesn't exist to see it."

He didn't have a response for that. He knew he'd insulted her, so of course she was going to look for proof to defend her position. But he also feared, just a little bit, that she could be right.

"Talk to Laura," she said softly. "Tell her the things you're feeling. She might talk back. And she might say things that surprise you."

If she said anything at all, that would surprise Jeremy. He was sure of that.

It was the only thing he was sure of right now.

Chapter Fifteen

Whitney was up before either of the other two. She had a crick in her neck and her tailbone hurt from sleeping sitting up against the cave wall again. There just wasn't enough room for all three of them to lie down, and the other two definitely needed it. Her clothes were still damp from the rain.

She got to see the sun rise, the forest green and glistening from a whole night of rain, the birds singing and frolicking. When she made her way to the edge of the cave, she saw two birds sitting on the tarp, dipping their beaks into the water and tossing it over their bodies.

Gross.

But beggars couldn't be choosers. Their choice was bird water or no water. She chose bird water. She noted that the two empties she'd left on the cave edge were each half-full of rainwater. She poured one into the other, and took the empties down the mountain. The birds scattered as she reached the tarp, and she couldn't help looking up, scanning for the woodpecker. She didn't see it anywhere.

She regretted having mentioned the woodpecker to Jeremy last night. She wasn't even sure why she'd done it. She meant what she'd said, but didn't understand why she'd needed to say it. And she was afraid of how he would respond to it in the light of day. Surely he would have questions.

She filled the empty bottles, then drank one and refilled it again, doing her best to ignore the dirt that had settled to the bottom. She hoped if the unclean water made them sick, they would at least be back home before it hit them. She capped the bottles and gave the tarp over to the birds.

"Go ahead," she called. "Don't let me interrupt your bath. But you could have at least asked if we were done with it yet." She smiled, feeling a little like a cartoon princess, talking to birds as if they were people. If only she had an army of helpful winged friends to lead her out of these woods. Or to lead a rescuer to her.

She sat on a nearby boulder and studied the forest, contemplating how *beautiful* and *dangerous* often went together, and how her fear of that combination was limiting her. She hadn't seen it. How long had she been keeping beauty at arm's length in hopes of avoiding danger? And how was that different from the way Jeremy approached his life? She and Cindy had been tsk-tsking over his actions, while conveniently ignoring their own.

She straightened her leg and stretched and rotated

her ankle. It was still terribly swollen, and it hurt like the dickens. But she could walk, and that was what was important for now. Hopefully, Jeremy would be able to walk on his.

In the morning silence, she could hear the far-off rumble of a helicopter. Once again, she told herself it was a search party coming for them, and once again she refused to allow her hopes to be dashed by the fact that it seemed far away. She imagined that Cindy was sitting in the cockpit, phone in hand, searching for the cave and tarp and crevasse Whitney had texted her about. She pretended that the people in the helicopter could see her, even if she couldn't see them.

She reached into her pocket and pulled out her phone.

Message failed.

Her heart sank with disappointment, but she was still able to pull up the image in her mind, and just thinking it made her feel better. She imagined her woodpecker guiding the helicopter their way, its little wings beating furiously on the current of the giant spinning blades, Rob with his binoculars, shouting, *Follow that bird*!

Her mother always told her that she expected too much, which was apparently a problem for people who lived with their heads in the clouds. If you had a big imagination, you could create scenarios that could never rationally come true. And then you wondered why they weren't happening. The real answer: because you made them up. Your disappointment was your own creation.

Because Jeremy is right and there are a million woodpeckers in the forest, and just because you've seen a couple of them does not make the woodpecker you've seen special. And it doesn't make you special, either, Whitney. It's a bird. Birds live in trees.

It's not fair *or* just *or* decent. *It just is.*

But when you spent a lot of time with your head in the clouds, how were you supposed to know what was imagination and what was real? Whitney didn't want to admit it, even to herself, that if she were also imagining her bond with Jeremy, she would be disappointed. Maybe even crushed.

It was about more than the fact that he was handsome. It was about more than how smart and dedicated he was. How understanding and tender he was with his daughter. His undying devotion to a promise he'd made to a woman who was long gone.

It was about a connection that she'd never felt with anyone before.

It seemed unlikely to feel that connection without the other person feeling it too, but Whitney supposed it was possible. When he'd placed his hand over hers, she'd trembled with emotion. So many things piling up inside of her. So many things she wanted to admit and was at the same time terrified to admit. She was touched that Jeremy opened up to her, even if what he had to say was difficult to hear.

She'd stayed up part of the night watching him. Trying to decide who this man was, and what it was about him that drew her to him. And, as if in answer to her thoughts, Sam whimpered, her eyelids flickering with dreams, and Jeremy stirred, turned and put his arm around his daughter protectively. Without opening his eyes, he shushed her, whispering to her until she calmed. Whitney wasn't even sure if he was awake, or if he was operating on pure love alone. He was so dedicated to the little girl, he didn't even need to be conscious to protect her.

It was a beautiful thing to witness, really.

Whitney kicked off her shoes and pulled off her socks, allowing her feet to feel air for the first time since this nightmare began. Her damp socks had turned her skin white and clammy, and she could see a stark "bruise sock" that began at the point where her ankle had been wrenched and stretched in both directions, ending somewhere around midfoot. She massaged it softly, breathing slowly in through her nose and out through her mouth. It didn't look good, but freedom from the shoes sure felt good.

The hum of the helicopter grew louder, and while she still couldn't see it, she almost thought she could spot its shadow moving over the leaves and forest floor off in the distance. She took comfort where she could get it: the helicopter was on the same side of the mountain that they were on. She squinted, waiting to see the blur of its blades, the lazy sway of the treetops, but never did. The disappointment was a blow that she tried not to feel.

A realization nearly stole her breath from her. This moment felt like a symbol for her life. Joy circled and circled, searching for her, but she was too guarded to get on board. Instead, she stayed under cover and massaged her bruises.

She thought about a conversation she'd had with her mom a year or so ago. She had just broken off a budding relationship with a man she'd met at a nursing conference. He was sweet and handsome and caring, and they always had fun, but their connection was lacking something that Whitney couldn't quite pinpoint. She was glum—not about losing him, but about losing the possibility of him.

Whitney, you have to let people in, her mom had said.

I let people in. I'm a nurse. I let people in all day.

No, no, I don't mean take on their pain. That's different. Take on their happiness. Take on your own happiness.

I'm happy. If you're worried about me being lonely—

That's exactly what I'm worried about.

Well, don't. I'm not lonely, Mom.

I don't want you to look back someday and wish you'd shared your life with someone else.

I shared my life with you. I'm still sharing it.

You're being unreasonable now.

I'm not.

Just promise me, okay? Humor me.

Promise you what? That I'll fall in love and get married like you and Dad?

She'd let the insinuation hang between them, mostly because she'd mentioned it a million times before and didn't need to say it aloud for her mother to hear it loud and clear: *That I'll be devastated when he dies, just like you were?*

Whitney. I know you're afraid of getting hurt. I hope that someday you'll get past that. I hope that you'll open yourself up to it.

At the time, Whitney had been offended—and completely confused—that her mother would even suggest such a thing. Who wanted their child to open themselves to hurt? And, sitting beside her mother's casket the evening before the funeral, she angrily swiped at tears, remembering that very conversation and thinking once again that if love was about this kind of hurt, she wanted nothing to do with it.

But after these past couple of days, she thought she might understand what her mother had been saying. It wasn't the hurt that was worth opening yourself to. It was all the good stuff that led up to it. You couldn't have one without the other.

She realized that, even though you didn't know it at the time, you were born with skin in the game. You loved your parents before you were aware how much it would hurt to sever that love. But you had to get on the field and play.

You had to open yourself to hurt.

You had to accept that you were developing feelings for the man in the cave above you, and that part of why you wanted so badly to get out of this darn forest was so you could explore those feelings further. So you could put real skin in the game.

There was a change in the sound of the helicopter,

and then a shadow swooped over Whitney. She looked up just in time to see the trees begin to sway, kicking tiny leaves and debris into her eyes. She blinked and shaded them with her hand but couldn't stop looking up. It was like she was looking at a dream.

The shadow turned to something more, and before she knew it, she could see the actual helicopter hovering over her.

She jumped up and waved her hands over her head. "Hey!" she shouted. "Hey! Down here! Help! Help!"

She pulled out her phone and frantically texted.

I can see you! You're right above me!

Please! Help us!

Get this text!

She watched as her phone kicked back message after message: message failed, message failed, message failed...

With a grunt, she tossed her phone to the ground and pulled the walkie-talkie out of her waistband.

"Rob! Are you there?" She waited, but only heard the whir of the helicopter. It seemed to be hovering in place. Maybe they did see her. Maybe Rob was receiving her message! "Rob! Rob! Come in! We're right here! You're right on top of us!" She frantically waved with her free arm while she talked.

But the radio never made a sound that she could hear. Rob never responded. She tried, over and over, for what seemed like a lifetime but was probably only a couple of minutes, while the helicopter slowly swayed around and then turned away from her. With a change in pitch of the motor, it flew away.

"No!" Whitney shouted. She pressed the button on the side of the walkie again. "No! Please! Don't go! We're here!"

She jumped off the rock and ran after the helicopter, shouting and waving the whole way, begging for them to see her or hear her or… Something. Anything! She followed its trajectory up the mountain, running, even though the back of her mind screamed to pay attention to the ground, lest she end up at the bottom of a cliff again.

She was no match in speed for a helicopter. It was soon a distant hum again, as it had been all morning, but desperation had taken over and she kept moving, kept churning her bare feet up the mountain, kept ignoring the sharp stab of rocks each time her step landed. She ran with her eyes on the machine's shadow, but even as she lost sight of it, the mountain terrain won again. She tripped over a rock and tumbled painfully to the ground, the walkie bouncing away from her.

"No!" she cried into the dirt, pounding her fist against it, not even aware of the scrapes on the bottoms of her feet. She didn't care enough to be aware. She was too devastated. "No!" she repeated. "Come back!"

It was as if a hurricane had filled her to bursting, the tears and words and anger and sadness screaming out of her in ragged cry after ragged cry that filled her lungs and emptied her soul.

She was only barely aware when a pair of arms wrapped themselves tight around her and helped her to sitting. Jeremy was on the ground next to her and pulled her toward him, shushing her the way he'd shushed Sam the night before.

"It's okay," he repeated. "It's okay, it's okay."

"It's not," she wailed into his shirt. "It's not okay. They were so close!"

"Maybe they saw us," he said. "Maybe they saw you and are making a plan to come back."

Whitney shook her head, wanting to be positive but feeling utterly miserable. It wasn't just that her rescue hopes had been dashed, it was that she'd finally figured out what her mother had meant and was ready to give it a try. She was ready to let someone in, and feared that her future in his arms would be short and sad and left in these woods. She'd gotten her skin on, and the game had been canceled.

Instead of arguing, though, she gave in to a pitiful sob, going limp against the ground. Jeremy let her go and settled for just sitting next to her, patting her back and murmuring hope that landed on deaf ears.

After what seemed like forever, Whitney sat up. Together, they watched the sky, Whitney's soft hiccups punctuating the buzz of the helicopter that softened as it got farther and farther away. Whitney knew they were both hoping to see it come back.

But eventually the hiccups were the only sound at all.

Chapter Sixteen

Whitney had pulled herself together before Sam woke up. She and Jeremy joked, a bit glumly, about how teenagers can sleep through anything, even a helicopter and a screaming woman. Even through her dad tumbling out of a cave, half-asleep, to get to the screaming woman quickly.

"I thought you were being attacked by a bear," he said.

Whitney froze. "Do you think there are bears?"

He chuckled. "Well, of course there are. This is Missouri. There are bears and bobcats and…" He pointed to his still-swollen leg.

"Lions and tigers, too?" Whitney asked. She'd laid her wet socks across a rock to dry and was flipping them over to the other side. No doubt about it, her impromptu run across the forest floor hadn't helped her ankle situation in the least, and she felt the need to have it bound by a sock and shoe again for stability. The ache was reaching all the way to her knee now.

"Oh, my," he said in a high-pitched voice, then followed it with, "No. I meant snakes."

"I know," she said. "You shouldn't have gone up that mountain, though. Especially half-asleep."

"And miss my chance to fend off a bear and be memorialized forever in the annals of hero history? I think not. Besides, you ran up that mountain."

"But your leg."

"But your ankle," he countered, and then his face darkened with a worry that he didn't seem to want to be admitting. "My leg will be fine," he said. "Just maybe not as fine as it used to be."

She studied it—the skin shiny and tight, a circle around the bite nearly black. He would lose tissue for sure. Had probably already lost it. But he could bear weight, and he didn't seem to feel shaky and weak anymore. He was no longer nauseous. Improvement.

Sam poked her head out the cave opening, and then came out, her hair mussed. "What are you guys doing out here?" she asked.

"Laundry," Whitney said with a thin smile, gesturing to her socks stretched out on the rock. She and Jeremy had already agreed not to tell Sam about the helicopter. No use getting her hopes up for nothing.

"I'm hungry," she said, flopping into Jeremy's lap, a motion that was so smooth and sure, Whitney guessed that it had happened a million times before.

"There are still a couple granola bars," Jeremy said.

She made a face. "I'm sick of granola bars. I want French fries. And pancakes."

"Together?" Jeremy asked.

Sam wrinkled her nose playfully. "Yeah. And a milkshake. And bacon."

"That's disgusting," he said.

"Is not!" Sam declared.

He flipped her sideways and began tickling her foot. "Is too!" he mocked in a high-pitched voice. Sam burst into contagious giggles that Whitney couldn't help sharing. Their relationship was sweet. And something seemed to have shifted inside of Jeremy overnight. He was lighter, funny, less worried and more hopeful. Their situation hadn't gotten any less dire, but he'd gotten less dire in his reaction to it.

A part of Whitney worried that this new change meant he'd given up.

She wasn't ready to give up.

"How about pig's feet and chocolate sauce instead?" Jeremy asked, letting Sam catch her breath.

She pushed her hair out of her face in a very little-girl fashion that reminded Whitney that Sam was still just on the cusp of becoming a teenager. Still a child. Many of the kids in the youth group straddled that line. They wanted to be cool and aloof, but every so often, the child inside would push toward the front, and Whitney always wished that they would stay that way for just a little longer. Once you let the adult take over completely, it was very hard to tap into that innocence again.

"I'll take the chocolate sauce," Sam said. "You eat the pig's feet." She said the word *feet* on a squealy giggle, rightly anticipating what Jeremy was going to do next. He flipped her sideways the other direction and tickled her other foot.

Normally, in a situation like this, Whitney felt like she was intruding somewhere she didn't belong. The bond between the two of them was truly something special, and Whitney could see the hard work that Jeremy put into being both mother and father for Sam. But something about them made her feel like part of the joke. Like they wanted her here. She busied herself shaking out her socks and putting them on while they goofed around. Every so often she would toss out a disgusting food match—chicken livers and gummy worms! Pop-Tarts and cat food!—and the giggling would renew once again.

Her sock felt even tighter against her ankle, and her shoe didn't want to go on. She idly thought that maybe she should just leave the shoe and sock off and embrace the fact that they weren't getting out of here. If, instead of the woodpecker, the real sign was the helicopter skimming and leaving. Just call this cave home now. Eat vegetation and drink rainwater and tell silly jokes while they waited to die, barefoot.

Stop it, Whitney, she told herself. *Don't be dramatic. You'll get out of this. You're a smart woman, and you know that the helicopter hovered in one spot for so long for a reason.*

And she did. It was something she didn't dare speak aloud, and a hope she hadn't even really let herself fully feel. Because if she was wrong and that hope was dashed again, she didn't know how she would react. How many times would she let this dumb forest knock her down before she just stopped getting back up?

Sam had gone back into the cave in search of the last few granola bars. Whitney's stomach felt as if it was turning itself inside out with hunger. But she knew Sam would need those granola bars more than she did. And she knew there was no way Jeremy would touch them as long as they were out here. He actually would eat a tree first.

"So…" Jeremy said, scanning the forest with his eyes. He'd stretched his bad leg in front of him.

"So?" Whitney echoed.

"What's today's plan? I don't know if either of us is in any condition to walk a great distance. Plus, the cave is good shelter, and I don't know if we'll be lucky enough to find another one. Sam thinks we should find a clearing, start a fire and hope someone sees the smoke."

"But what happens if the fire gets away from us? It could burn down the whole forest. And us in it."

"Okay," he said, nodding, as if she'd reconfirmed his thoughts.

Whitney tied her shoes. "I was thinking. In our training, we went over what to do if we got lost on the hike."

Whitney remembered the kids making fun of the video they'd shown. The actors were so melodramatic. *There's like, literally a path*, she remembered one of the kids saying. *How do you get lost on a path?* They'd done their best to shush the kids, but when one of the actors threw up his hands and exclaimed, *We've been walking in circles this whole time!* they burst out laughing, and even Whitney herself had joined in with a chuckle or two. It had seemed ridiculous.

She wanted to laugh and cry at that memory now. She agreed it was wise to make the kids watch the dramatic video just so they could say they'd covered all bases. But secretly she'd thought the kids were right—if you stayed on the path, it was almost impossible to get lost. But here they were, lost. They had walked in circles. They had slipped over cliff edges and into crevasses and been bitten by snakes.

All in all, pretty dramatic.

So dramatic, in fact, she hadn't even thought about that video until this morning when she was racking her brain for a solution to their problem.

"I remember," Jeremy said.

"They said if you get lost in the woods, you should just stay put. The more you move, the harder you are to find."

Jeremy nodded, taking this in. "I remember that, too," he said. "It's hard for me to just sit around waiting, though. I feel like I need to be doing something."

"We'll do things," Whitney said. "We'll yell. We'll keep trying the walkie-talkie."

He scanned the forest again, his eyes lighting on a plateau just a few feet away and above them. "If I go up there, maybe I'll get a better view. Maybe I'll be able to see a trail. Or the spotter in the helicopter will see me."

"Can you get up there on that leg?" Whitney asked.

He pulled himself to standing and brushed off the back of his pants. "I think I can."

"So is that the plan, then?" Whitney asked.

He limped closer to her and held out his hand. She took it and let him pull her to her feet. Her heart lurched into second gear as she stood in front of him. He held her hand even though she was standing now. For the longest time they just stood and looked at each other. There was a softness to Jeremy's features that she hadn't noticed until now when she was up close. His jaw didn't seem so set with three days of stubble on it. His eyes didn't seem so wary. He wasn't standing with balled fists. His posture was more relaxed.

Trembling, Whitney reached out and touched his cheek with one finger. "You're getting a beard."

He laughed and looked at the ground, and she was pretty sure she saw a blush color the tops of his cheeks, his forehead. "Not too many razors in the forest, it turns out," he said. "I'm going for a new look—mountain wanderer."

Whitney wondered what she looked like right now. Dirty, limping, her clothing torn, braids unkempt and unwashed. She was sure she looked no more put together than Jeremy or Sam, but she also knew that it didn't matter.

"I like it," she said. She smoothed a braid. "I'm going for the same look. I think it'll be all the rage in Hollywood this year."

He chuckled again. "You're funny," he said, as if he'd only just realized this for the first time. As if this was a big revelation for him.

Whitney did a silly little curtsy, still keeping her hand in his, afraid that if she removed it, he would never take it again, and his palm just felt too warm and wonderful to let go. She licked her lips nervously.

"Can I ask you a question?" she asked.

"Sure."

She felt nearly bowled over with a woozy wave of nerves and fear and chemistry. She understood now why they called it *falling* in love—because in some ways, it really did feel like falling. Uncontrolled, scary, exhilarating.

She was pretty sure that Jeremy was experiencing the same terrifying exhilaration—she could feel it beating through his palm and into hers—but now that she had his attention, she wasn't sure she wanted to ask anymore. It felt too risky, too real.

She swallowed, her throat feeling dry again, even though she'd drunk her share of rainwater. She could hear herself breathing, and over that, she could hear him breathing, too. They were close enough to be breathing the same air, a thought that made her feel heavy and rooted and as if they would land their fall on the same spot. She might never let go of his hand ever again.

"Do you…" She couldn't go on. Her breath and her boldness had been stolen away at the thought of his answer.

"Do I…?" he prodded.

"Do you…feel it, too?"

He didn't answer for so long, embarrassment and dread began to build up in her. His lips parted, but nothing came out. She felt it, whatever "it" was that was coursing between them, electricity from one sweaty hand to another. But what if she was wrong? She'd never felt this way before and could have been misinterpreting it as something else entirely. What if she'd just made a total fool of herself? The longer he paused, the surer she was that she had.

"I…" he started, but at that same moment, Sam poked her head out of the cave again.

"Gum!" she called triumphantly, waving a small silver package in the air.

Jeremy's grasp loosened, and Whitney took that as her chance to step away, break the… Whatever it was. Because clearly he didn't feel it the same way that she did, and now she was burning with humiliation.

Really, Whitney, you think you're just going to accidentally get stranded in a forest with the love of your life? Is that how it's going to go? How naive! You really fell for that open-yourself-up nonsense hook, line and sinker, didn't you?

But from far away she heard a familiar laughing call—the call of a woodpecker, followed by the wooden knock of a beak against bark.

Oh, how convenient. So convenient, it's clearly all in your head, too, she thought glumly.

Sam scrambled up the rocky hill with an agility that made Whitney suck in a breath, sure the little girl would face-plant the same way that she had. But instead, Sam ran to Jeremy and Whitney brandishing the small package.

"You had gum in one of the side pockets," she said.

"Oh, I forgot," Jeremy said.

"There's lots left," Sam said thrusting the pack at Whitney. "Here, take a piece."

Whitney never thought spearmint could taste so good. Or be such a good distraction.

Chapter Seventeen

"There's no coverage up here, either," Jeremy called. He'd finally made it to the flat spot above the cave, which had required him to do a little rock climbing with no gear and with his balance thrown off. The spot had looked like a shelf from below, but really was little more than a ledge. He didn't want to tell Whitney and Sam that, though. They would both worry. And they might be right. He couldn't put much weight on his leg at all without the bite burning.

A breeze ruffled his hair, making him aware of how claustrophobic the forest was, even if it was outside. He felt more clearheaded up here. He could think.

Autumn was more present from above. He knew this. He'd driven the highways through the mountains hundreds of times before and could picture the rolling trees vividly. What was massive from within seemed small from another perspective. Something for him to remember.

The leaves were turning fast and would be falling soon. If it kept raining every night, the combination of water and dead leaves could prove to be even more dangerous. But by then they would be out of here. That, he was promising himself.

Whitney had given him her cell phone, and he'd taken his own. He marveled at the pink, glittery case on her phone. Something he would have expected on Sam's phone. Similar to the glittery sunglasses that had started their journey into the forest to begin with. It seemed whimsical, childlike. That was one of the things he'd first noticed about Whitney, though, wasn't it? Her playful side. Her innocence. His mother would have called her a breath of fresh air. He would have added the word *needed* there—a *needed* breath of fresh air. One of those things you didn't realize you desperately craved until you got it.

Both phones were getting zero bars, plus Whitney's battery was nearly dead. The phones had never been a lifeline to the outside world, but the thought of them dying somehow made things feel more final. Another possibility for rescue taken away. He didn't think they could afford to lose too many more of those. If they didn't get out of this forest soon, he doubted that they would.

She was right, of course. Staying put was the right idea. He didn't need to watch some soap opera–style video to know that. But staying in one place was hard. It felt like they were doing nothing. Doing nothing was against everything Jeremy believed in. Plus, he felt responsible for all of them. Even though Whitney and Sam were both strong and had already proven they could take care of themselves and each other, he still felt the pressure of getting them out of here. Although he wasn't quite sure if the motivation was driven by some sense of duty or something else. He suspected it was the latter.

Whitney's question—*Do you feel it, too?*—had taken him by surprise. Yes, he'd felt it. Of course he'd felt it. But he hadn't known that she did. Or maybe he'd known she did but hadn't thought she would call it out. Another thing to appreciate about Whitney— she said what was on her mind. If she ever silently brooded, he sure hadn't seen it. The closest had been that woodpecker thing.

And what was that even about? Inside, he agreed that yes, absolutely, a bird coming to you out of no- where and staring you down was… Not normal. But then what about this entire trip was even close to normal?

He pulled out the walkie-talkie and turned it on. Fiddled with the knobs a bit, trying to get something. Even the tiniest signal would be a positive step in the right direction. But, though he thought maybe he got a blip of something, he never got anything reliable. He sent out calls anyway.

"Hello? Rob? Cindy? This is Jeremy. Do you hear me? Hello?"

Down below, Whitney and Sam were folding the tarp, having drained the last of the rainwater into bottles that they kept out of the sun in the cave. Sam was talking Whitney's ear off, of course. School, boys, TV shows—you name it, his daughter had an opinion on it. Or a story to tell about it. She'd always been a talker, but the closer she got to her teen years, the more she seemed to chatter. It could get exhausting—Jeremy knew that firsthand—but Whitney seemed to enjoy the conversation. It was only the worried glances that she flicked at him every now and again that reminded him she was aware that they were stuck in a bad situation and weren't folding laundry in someone's living room.

Sam was currently talking to her about food. All the food she planned to eat when she got home. And a boy who she planned to talk to when she got back to school. All the homework she would need to get caught up on. Sam, optimistic that they would find a way to get home and she would soon be back at school. More optimistic than he was, that was for sure.

"Hello! Anyone there?" he said into the walkie, but again nothing.

He listened as they finished folding the tarp, and then Sam went into the cave and tossed out the backpack. He listened as Whitney unzipped the pack, telling Sam a story about when she was in middle school—a completely charming story about fighting, and winning, a war against administration to start a cupcake club. Cupcakes Are People Too! was her slogan, a saying so ridiculous Sam fell to the ground with laughter. Sam asked her if they ate people in that club, which prompted Whitney to start singing "Purple People Eater" for Sam, which devolved into a debate about whether the one-eyed, one-horned beast was purple, or if it was the people it ate that were purple. And where did purple people come from, anyway?

These were exactly the kinds of conversations Laura had with Sam. So easy, a single thought-flow that was part hilarity, part history, part education. When he tried for hilarity, he slipped into "dad jokes," which was apparently a whole thing now. When he went for history, he was boring. When he strove for education, he became a lecturer. At least that was how he felt.

"Hello! Anyone copy?" he asked into the walkie again. He turned a slow circle, looking for the helicopter.

"Wait a minute," he heard below him. "Jeremy!" Whitney was holding the small square of folded survival blanket. "I didn't even think about this."

"Think about what?"

She shook the blanket out and flipped it over. "It's silver!"

He screwed up his eyebrows in confusion, but then it dawned on him. Mylar. Silver. Of course.

"It never even registered with me that this was silver," she said.

"I don't get it," Sam said.

But Jeremy and Whitney were doing that thing again—where they were saying full sentences with their eyes. Whole, complete thoughts without speaking a single word.

"Reflective," he said. "It'll reflect the sun. Someone from above might see it shining."

Whitney nodded and sprang into motion. "Sam, help me spread this out. Get the ropes and the knife."

Whitney and Sam began spreading the blanket out, securing one corner with his knife and working to tie the others to nearby trees to keep them secure. They had moved closer to the rock face and were directly beneath him now. A space with few trees to obstruct the view from the air.

Now they just needed to get that helicopter back.

"Anyone hear me? Look for the reflective blanket. A silver square. You find it, you'll find us."

Chapter Eighteen

It had been hours since they set the blanket out, and still no helicopter. Whitney was now sure that thinking it had hovered above them for a reason was wrong. It was just searching. Clearly it found nothing. If it was even there to search for them at all. Maybe it was one of those recreational helicopter tour things. *See the spectacular fall foliage from above!*

The sun had warmed them a little, but she could hear the wind in the tops of the trees, a shushing sound that warned of possible bad weather again. It tended to happen this way in Missouri—days of rain followed by more days of rain; days of drought followed by more days of drought. Missouri weather could be volatile, but there was no such thing as a rainy season here. Of course, there was a first time for everything.

First time for getting stranded on a mountain.

First time for falling in love with the man you were stranded with. And his daughter.

Sam had grown quiet. For what seemed like hours, the girl had softly sung to herself. Whitney had begun to think she had sung herself to sleep, but every so often she would hear Sam whisper something to herself, or hear a sniffle, or watch a thrown pebble skitter off into the distance. What had originally seemed like a strange version of housekeeping had turned into a grim acceptance that yet another day was being stolen from them. Another day of getting weaker, thirstier, hungrier, more hopeless. Another day of worrying about bobcats and snakes and bears and rain and cold.

Jeremy was sitting above them, legs dangling over the ledge, the radio in his lap. Her phone had gone dead and he'd tossed it down to her and she'd silently cried over it, which seemed so unwarranted and so warranted all at the same time. At least when it had a battery there was a chance—no matter how remote—that she would make contact with someone. Now it was impossible. Message failed, forever.

"My mom smelled like coconuts," Sam said, interrupting Whitney's thoughts. At first Whitney wasn't sure if Sam was still talking to herself or if she meant to get Whitney's attention. But then Sam turned to her side and rested her head on one elbow so she was facing Whitney. "I'm pretty sure it was her shampoo. I can't remember, and Dad says he doesn't remember, but I definitely remember the smell. Coconuts, and sometimes when she and Dad were going on date nights, peaches and flowers."

Whitney offered her an encouraging smile. "That sounds like a lovely combination." She understood the power of a mother's scent, and knew that if she got a whiff of lilac perfume, her mother would be as alive in her mind as she ever was.

"The guy who killed her was a stranger. Did you know that part? That she was killed?"

Whitney nodded. "Yes. I'm sorry. It's a terrible thing."

Sam picked apart a leaf, pensive. "She was probably thinking about me when she died, though. My dad thinks so. I think so, too."

"I'm sure she was," Whitney said. She wasn't sure if Sam was hearing her responses, or if she was even meant to respond at all. Maybe Sam just needed to purge some thoughts. Whitney definitely understood that need.

"My dad is lonely," Sam said. "He doesn't want me to know that, but I know it anyway. I can tell." This time Whitney really didn't know what to say, so she said nothing. "He's never had a date since Mom died. He just goes to work and comes home and goes to work and comes home and goes to work and comes home…" She tossed her head side to side to show the monotony of it all. "It's kind of depressing."

Whitney was struck with the realization that she really didn't do much more than that herself. Sure, every so often she and Cindy would meet for dinner or a quick Saturday afternoon bike ride. She had church, and the youth group. She was friendly with the other nurses, but they were hardly buddies. Not the kind that got together to do things. And she couldn't remember her last date. It had been at least a year. She just hadn't been interested. It seemed nobody out there was made for her.

Until now.

"Sounds like he works really hard," Whitney said.

"But he never has any fun. And he doesn't think I notice that every day he looks sadder." She pulled herself to sitting, crossed her legs and picked up a leaf to shred. "And maybe I didn't notice—like, *really* notice—until now. But it's hard not to see it when I watch the way he is around you. Even though we're stuck in a forest."

Whitney wanted to glance at Jeremy, to see if he was hearing this, but at the same time was glad that he was behind her, which spared her the embarrassment she was feeling. It seemed that Sam thought she was talking to just Whitney, but she was definitely talking loudly enough for him to hear. It felt too personal to acknowledge in the moment. She kept her eyes on the ground in front of her.

"When he looks at you, he has happy eyes."

"Happy eyes?" It popped out before Whitney could stop herself.

Sam nodded and drew lines on the corners of her eyes with her fingers. "They get all squinty and sparkly and like, wrinkly at the edges. Kind of like when he laughs. I always called them his happy eyes. I know that sounds dumb and like something a little kid would say, but it's true. I remember. He used to have those eyes with my mom. I wish he had them more often. Like, if we weren't lost on a mountain, his eyes would probably be super squinty and wrinkly around you."

Again, Whitney was tempted to glance at Jeremy, to have one of their unspoken conversations, but she couldn't make herself do it. Part embarrassment, part fear. What if he denied everything Sam was saying, and she could see it on his face? What if Whitney had been imagining things all along?

"I'm sure he's just glad that we found you and that you're okay," Whitney said, but she kept her voice low, just in case he was hearing this and was as aware of her feelings as she was.

"That's probably part of it," Sam said. Whitney was surprised by how disappointed she felt at her own theory being validated. She wanted Sam to be right.

"We're both glad about that," Whitney said. "Very glad. Even though we're not particularly happy about…the whole situation."

"Yeah," Sam said. She was looking at something far away over Whitney's shoulder. Or maybe far away in time. It was hard to tell which. They were both silent for a long while, Sam staring at whatever it was she was seeing and Whitney thinking about Jeremy's *happy eyes*. What did those eyes look like at the end of the workday? On a weekend walking hand in hand around a lake? In a cabin on summer vacation? In every scenario, they filled her with longing.

"Can I tell you a secret?" Sam crawled across the blanket toward her. Whitney held the corner nearest her—the one not secured to the ground—so it wouldn't scrunch up under the movement. Sam looked younger then. Whitney could imagine her as a toddler, crawling for the first time. How cute she must have been. Sam plopped herself in front of Whitney so close that their knees were touching.

Whitney pushed a piece of Sam's dirty hair behind her ear. Some of it was stuck in the dried blood that had seeped out from under the now-filthy bandages Whitney had covered her wound with. The girl's lips were dry again, chapped. Whitney began to wonder how long they would be able to go on the rainwater she'd collected, how long before one of them succumbed to an infection. She hoped against hope that it would rain again tonight so they could drink tomorrow, and that the ointment she'd found would fend off the worst of the bacteria. But her hollow stomach reminded her that soon she would have more problems than just thirst and surface wounds.

And the thought about them doing anything out here tomorrow was almost more than she could take. She had to lock it out of her mind. Concentrate on the girl in front of her.

"Sure," she said, offering Sam a warm smile, because the girl definitely did not need to know about Whitney's fears and worries. She'd shouldered enough adult things in her life already.

Sam glanced upward, toward Jeremy, and Whitney followed her glance. He was standing now, with his back to them, looking through his binoculars at something they couldn't see from their vantage point. Maybe he hadn't heard any of this, a thought that both relieved and disappointed Whitney. She wanted him to hear, to confirm it by saying nothing.

Sam licked her lips, which did nothing to wet them, renewing Whitney's worry. "I want a mom again." She gazed at Whitney with such raw honesty, it nearly broke Whitney's heart. "I mean, I miss my mom. But she's been gone a long time, and it's just me and Dad. And she's my mom, but I don't really remember much about her. So it's kind of like she was never real. Does that make sense?" Whitney nodded. "I want a *mom* again. I know it won't be like, my real mom. But still. I miss having a whole family." She looked down at her lap and brushed away a leaf that had fallen onto her leg. "Is that dumb? Do you think my mom would be mad? Or like, disappointed?"

"Of course it's not dumb," Whitney said, ducking so she could get in Sam's gaze. "It's not dumb at all." *I miss it, too*, she wanted to say, but found that she couldn't get those words out. "I didn't know Laura, but she sounds like a wonderful person, and I think she would understand."

"I know my dad is afraid that I'll really like someone he dates and then if it doesn't work out or something, I'll be upset. And that's part of why he's not dating. He doesn't want me to lose a mom twice. I heard him tell my grandma that. But he doesn't understand. I already lost my mom. Nothing else will ever come close. And I would rather have someone to love and lose than nobody at all."

Whitney's breath had been sucked out of her. Had she not been battling her own loneliness using those very same words? It was too painful, she'd thought. The loss was too hard. But was it really? Would she have given up a single second of her life with her mother if she'd known that she was going to lose her long before she was ready?

Absolutely not.

Silly, Whitney thought. *You would have never been ready. You were always going to lose her before you wanted to. That's how it goes. But you would never have given up a single day. A single shopping trip. A single lemon cheesecake.*

"Anyway," Sam said, "sometimes when I say my prayers, I ask my mom to bring someone into my dad's life. Do you think she would do that?"

Whitney nodded. If she thought her mother would send a woodpecker to her for some reason she didn't even understand, she definitely thought Sam's mom could find a way to answer Sam's prayer.

But then that begged the question—was she the answer to someone's prayer? That seemed like a big stretch, not to mention a tall order. And a responsibility she didn't quite know what to do with. If you were the answer to someone's prayers, what happened if you didn't measure up?

"I know this sounds crazy, but when I see his happy eyes, I kind of wonder if she heard my prayers and if you're that person." Now Sam's face flushed and she ducked away from Whitney's gaze, as if she'd put herself too far out there and wasn't sure how Whitney would respond. As if she was fearful that Whitney would tell her that she was crazy or silly or that she didn't like Jeremy that way.

But she did like him that way.

After a long, uncomfortable pause, during which Whitney's mind searched every possible response, she said, "I do like your dad, but it may be too soon to know if I'm that person." Her cheeks felt flushed after having said it, and she longed so much to look over her shoulder to see if Jeremy had heard. She felt like a middle schooler again—*does he or doesn't he like me, too?*

Whitney was more than aware that Jeremy and Sam were a package deal. Letting Jeremy in would be committing something to Sam, and though she didn't know what exactly that commitment was, she was certain she could make it. She loved the girl. That love was important.

"Have you ever prayed for something, and then had it come true?" Sam asked.

Whitney thought about it. More times than she could count, she'd prayed for something that later happened exactly as she'd asked for it to happen. Had it been a result of her prayer, or had it been coincidence? Of course, nobody knew for sure. But Whitney knew. That was the nature of faith. Or at least the nature of her faith. The knowing. The believing.

She sorely wished Jeremy had that knowing. She wanted that peace for him.

"Yes," Whitney said, feeling a little like she couldn't catch her breath. "All the time."

Sam touched the bandaged wound on her head as

she looked around the forest, as if seeing it for the first time. "I just want to get out of here," she said in a small voice.

"Me, too," Whitney said, also taking in the trees and brush that wanted to press in on her, making her feel surrounded if she let it. The spell had been broken. Sam had gotten the comfort she'd needed in that moment. Whitney wondered if part of that comfort was just in knowing that someone *could* love her dad again, that she *could* be part of a whole family again, even if they would never get out of here to enjoy it.

"What do you miss most?" Sam curled up on her side again, folding her hands together under her cheek and pulling her knees up to her chest. She looked like a child who was tired at the end of a holiday.

Whitney didn't have a chance to respond before Sam kept talking.

"I miss my friends. Lily especially. Do you miss your best friend?"

Whitney nodded. "Yes. I miss Miss Cindy a lot." It was the truth. She was pretty sure she and Cindy would have a whole spa day together when Whitney got home. *If...*her brain tried to correct, but Whitney shoved the thought away. *Not if. When.*

"We made friendship bracelets on the bus, but we put them in her backpack, so I don't have mine. Do you think she would give mine to someone else?"

"No," Whitney said. "Absolutely not. Plus, it won't matter. You're going to get out of here and wear it yourself."

Sam nodded contemplatively. "I also miss ice

cream," she said. "What's your favorite flavor? Mine's blueberry, but you never see it anywhere. Always chocolate or vanilla. Boring."

Whitney chuckled. "Well, I was just getting ready to say my favorite is chocolate, but…"

"Ugh! Boring!" Sam said, and her voice tried to be animated, but she seemed too tired to really pull it off. Whitney began ticking through the things that could cause her fatigue. Head wound…dehydration… hypoglycemia…too many choices for Whitney's comfort. "My dad likes chocolate, too. Oh, you know what else I miss?" Whitney didn't respond. She knew she didn't need to. "Movies. Do you like movies? My dad has like, a zillion movies."

Whitney opened her mouth to respond but realized that this wasn't just a list of all the things Sam missed; it was a checklist to see if Whitney and Jeremy were as good a match as it seemed. "A zillion, huh?" Whitney finally said. "I'll bet there are lot in his collection that I've never seen."

"Probably." Sam's eyes had drifted to half-mast, and Whitney tried to keep her worry at bay. "I'm getting tired. We should take naps."

"Okay," Whitney said. She scooted so that she could lie across from Sam, mirroring her fetal pose, her back to Jeremy, her knees almost touching Sam's knees. She didn't close her eyes, though.

"I miss my phone," Sam said.

"I miss mine, too," Whitney admitted.

She saw a tear snake out of Sam's closed eye and pool into the crease of her nose. A matching tear slipped down the side of her face and soaked into the blanket beneath her.

"I miss my mom," Sam whispered.

"I miss mine, too," Whitney whispered back, two matching tears snaking their way down her cheeks, as well.

Sam's breath evened out, and Whitney began to feel a tug at her eyelids, sleep pushing in on her. She became aware of how dry her own lips were. How the aching in her ankle seemed a dull pulse throughout her entire body. How her stomach suddenly felt too full, even though it was so empty it had recently been cramping in on itself. This wasn't good, she knew, and she wondered if Jeremy was faring the same, but her head felt too heavy to turn and check on him.

"Whitney?" Sam whispered.

Her eyes flew open, her heart kick-starting, as if she'd been caught sleeping on the job. "Yeah?"

"Can we pray?"

"Sure." Whitney slowly, slowly pulled herself to sitting, although Sam stayed exactly like she was. "Do you want to lead the prayer, or do you want me to?"

"I want to," Sam said. Her voice was so faint. It was hard to believe that this was the same kid who'd only minutes before been talking about the things she was missing.

Whitney clasped her hands together and bowed her head, and it seemed like she stayed that way forever before Sam started talking. So long, she'd started to wonder if Sam had fallen asleep, or if she'd maybe meant silent prayer. But just as Whitney opened her mouth to say the words, "Heavenly Father—"

"Please help us," Sam said in her clear, childlike voice. "We've done everything, God, and we're still stuck here. Please help. We don't want to die."

Whitney was struck by how simple and plainspoken the prayer was. No *thee* or *thy*, no lengthy proclamations of loyalty. Just a plea to Father from child. Help us. Please. "Amen," Whitney said, barely above a whisper.

"Also, God?" Sam said. "Please let my dad fall in love again. He's lonely. And I'm lonely. And Mom wouldn't want us to be lonely. Just ask her. I know she'll tell you that I'm right. He's done so much for me, God, but it's time for him to do something for him. So let him fall in love again. Especially if I…" She paused, and Whitney saw more tears flow. Her heart wrenched and tears tumbled down her face as she shut her eyes again, concentrating on the prayer. "Especially if I die. He'll take that really hard, God. And he's the world's best dad, so you have to protect him if that happens. He'll forget that he needs love, too. He already does forget that. Make sure he's not alone."

"Amen," Whitney whispered again.

"And if we all have to die, God…please just don't let it hurt too much. I think I can take it, but I don't think Dad could take watching it."

Whitney felt heavy and sad, as if someone were pulling on her from the inside. Sam had clearly thought about so many things that Whitney had not yet even considered. Things that would weigh heavily on anyone.

"Okay, God, is it okay if I talk to Mom for a second?" Sam opened one eye, and whispered, as if she was on hold in the middle of an important phone call. "Don't worry, I do this all the time. God's cool with it."

"I know," Whitney said. "I've been doing it a lot, too."

Sam closed her eye again and her brow furrowed with concentration. "Mom? It's Samantha. I'm pretty sure you've been watching everything, so you know that it's really bad. Not like your mom getting killed at work kind of bad, but close. That's not supposed to make you feel guilty or anything—I mean, I know you didn't want to get shot at work. Anyway, I was hoping you could maybe work on Dad a little? You know how sometimes you whisper to me in my dreams? Maybe you could do the same to Dad. Tell him it's okay to do fun things. Tell him everything is going to be all right." She took a deep breath. "Unless it's not going to be all right. I already mentioned this to God, but I figure as many people as I can get on the job, the better. If I die, will you meet me at…well, at where you go when you die? I think it's like a bridge or a doorway or something, but I don't know for sure, and you do. It would be pretty cool to see you. And if we all die, there will be this girl Whitney with us. You'll like her. I think Dad does. She kind of…" She hesitated, then her brow furrowed even deeper. "She kind of reminds me of you."

Whitney was certain she went a full thirty seconds without breathing.

"Okay, I'm sure that's pretty much everything," Sam said. She opened one eye again. "Except the Lord's Prayer."

Whitney nodded, then mouthed the words along with Sam. "Our Father who art in heaven…" but she had to admit to herself she wasn't paying attention. She was too curious. Did Jeremy hear any of this? Did he hear all of it? What did he think? Was he up there trying to come up with ways to let both Whitney and Sam down easy? Whitney vowed to herself that she would not talk to him about any of it. Let him believe she was neutral. Even though she wasn't.

She heard a knocking noise and opened her eyes. A woodpecker—no, *the* woodpecker, her gut told her— was standing on a nearby branch, craning its neck to stare at her, as if it had only knocked to get her attention. She watched as it hopped up and down the length of the branch, all the while keeping its eye on her.

"Give us this day…" she mouthed, although she was too distracted to really know what she was saying. The bird crouched and then lifted into the air, as if satisfied that it had made its point. But Whitney wasn't sure yet if she understood what exactly it was trying to tell her. "…and forgive us our trespasses…"

She watched as the bird flew in a tight circle, then lit on the same branch. Within seconds, it had lifted off again, flying closer to Whitney. It briefly landed on a closer branch. And then up and landed again, only this time on a nearby rock.

Mom? she thought once again. *It really is you, isn't it?* The bird hopped closer, stretched and bobbed, all while watching her. Suddenly she was hit with a wave of sadness and nostalgia. She missed her mom more than she could ever have imagined. An ache so deep it felt like it had taken up permanent residence inside her. She almost thought she could feel both her pain and Sam's, intertwined into one huge knot of insecurity.

Memories flooded her. She was six, standing on a kitchen chair, decorating sugar cookies, her mother's delicate hands sprinkling jimmies into the icing over her shoulder. She was eight, learning how to polka at a silly German restaurant, her mother's hand clasped around hers, their laughter intermingling. She was fifteen, crying over the broken heart of losing her father, her face stuffed into the familiar comforting scent of her mother's shirt, feeling the warm patter of her mother's tears on the top of her head—a literal rain of comfort. She was graduating middle school, graduating high school, graduating college, every single time picking her mother's face out of the crowd instantly, warmed by the proud swell in her mother's chest, the emotion behind her wave and blown kiss. She was on a hundred vacations and water parks and zoo trips and museum tours and shopping excursions and movie nights.

She felt crushed under the weight of all the memories. Almost as if, without having had the love of her mother, she would have done none of those things at all. The love and the loss were the same—without

one, you couldn't have the other. To choose to protect yourself from one was to choose to lose both,
and Whitney knew now that it was a choice she was
not willing to make.

"...as we forgive those who trespass against us..."
Whitney was aware that she'd nearly stopped mouth-
ing the words, as she was overcome with the urge to
touch the woodpecker. She unfolded her hands and
reached out. Reached, reached. She came within cen-
timeters before it took off again, this time looping
right over her head. She turned to watch it go.

And the rest of the prayer dried up in her mouth.
She didn't even hear it, as if Sam had simply faded
away.

The woodpecker landed on a jutting rock right
next to Jeremy. He was down on one knee—his good
knee—with his head bowed and hands pressed together. Even from below, Whitney could see the tears
streaming from his eyes, just as they had from hers
and Sam's. She could hear his voice murmuring the
prayer along with his daughter, the same echo that
she'd heard during "Happy Birthday" the night before.

They came to the end of the prayer, and in what
seemed like slow motion, Whitney watched as Jeremy slowly lifted his head, opened his eyes and gazed
right down at her. So many conversations passing
between them, all at once, as if their entire histories
were spilling directly into each other. As if their entire futures were, too.

They say if you see a woodpecker, you need to

pay attention. You know, opportunity is knocking, and all that.

Whitney watched as Jeremy slowly wiped his face with the palm of his hand, then looked to the sky, and said, loud and clear…

"Amen."

Chapter Nineteen

It seemed impossible, but they fell asleep. All of them. Jeremy had come down from the rock ledge and wrapped his arm around Sam, and the sun had reflected off the blanket, warming them. There was no sign of bad weather to come. *At least we won't die in the rain*, Jeremy thought bleakly before slipping into sleep. After Sam's prayer, he felt alarmingly accepting of his fate, although admittedly sad. He wasn't ready to die yet. He would never be ready to watch Sam die. And then there was Whitney. A wonderful complication in all of this.

Lying across from each other, Jeremy and Whitney had said nothing aloud; had only stared into each other's eyes until they'd faded out, all of the things they'd mutually come to accept understood and unspoken.

Sam was the first one snoring. Whitney was a close second. And then Jeremy had reluctantly let go.

Laura came to him in his dream. Not the Laura he'd last seen when he'd had to identify her body, which didn't look like Laura at all. So blue and cold and rigid. Jeremy had found it so interesting—so terrifying—how quickly a *person* became a *body* after death. A vessel that no longer carried anything. An empty cup. Seeing his wife as that empty cup had drained him in every conceivable way. At their age, it was still foreign to visualize each other as elderly; he'd certainly never visualized her as gone.

This Laura, the one in his dream, was warm and vibrant, her skin and hair glowing. She was wearing his favorite dress—a green wraparound that she'd picked up on their honeymoon in Cancun. It highlighted the red in her hair. Turned her skin rosy, like a holiday. She'd only worn it one time, to an intimate dinner on the edge of the ocean, which was invisible but noisy in the night. So beautiful, she had taken his breath away.

She came to him with a radiant smile that sent jolts of happiness through him.

"You did it," she said, never losing that smile.

"Did what?" he asked.

She reached out and touched his cheek. "I'm so proud of you."

"Did what?" he asked again. "What are you proud of?"

She responded with more of the same wide, knowing smile. She reached up with her other hand and placed it on his other cheek, then leaned in and hugged him, a sensation of completeness that he'd forgotten, but when she pulled away, her absence felt like physical pain.

He wanted more than anything to fill that empty space again but knew instantly that he couldn't fill it with the familiar warmth of Laura. He reached for her, tried to grasp her arm, but his hand clutched nothing, snapping itself into a fist. He plucked at an auburn curl that bounced against her shoulder, but his fingers pinched air.

He opened his mouth to object, to cry, to… Do something, he just didn't know what. Those things didn't seem right. Nothing seemed right. There was a distance between them that he'd finally become fully aware of. She was an empty cup, but he wasn't. Not yet. He was still alive, but he was only half-full.

She retreated a step, then two, then three. He wanted to follow her, but he knew he couldn't. He knew he wouldn't be happy where she was. Their happiness together was so complete. But it was fleeting. And it was over. Not in his heart. Not completely. Not ever. He would carry that happiness around in his store of memories for as long as he remained alive.

But there were still memories to be made. Just not with her. He knew this. And the empty part of him ached with that knowledge. He wanted more than anything to make it go away.

"I want—" he said, feeling the need to confess.

"You will," she said, her smile brightening. "You definitely will."

Jeremy snapped awake, an indignant cry on his lips that zipped away the moment his eyes opened.

Whitney lay across from him, her eyes fluttering beneath her eyelids as she dreamed her own injustices.

She was beautiful. She was smart and energetic, and she and Sam seemed to have created quite a bond. He'd heard Sam's words with his own two ears. She wanted him to move on. She wanted him to feel free to love. She especially wanted him to feel free to love Whitney. He and Sam had always been on the same wavelength when it came to important life decisions. He hadn't wanted to love again. Until now. But now he definitely did. Sam could see in him what he felt for Whitney, probably even before he had seen it.

You will. You definitely will.

He will, what? Love again?

Had Laura been letting him go in that dream? Had she been answering Sam's prayer? Answering his prayer?

A day ago, he would have said that was impossible. Hooey. But a day ago he would have said praying would be impossible. Now… It seemed more than possible. It seemed probable. It seemed necessary. His heart thrummed with longing, not just for Whitney, but for what having Whitney in his life could mean. His heart thrummed for the future.

Whitney stirred, and he noticed that wisps of her hair had lifted from her temple and begun dancing in the air. Sam's, too, an errant lock reaching backward and tickling his nose. He felt a breeze and hoped that it didn't mean a storm was rolling in after all. He wanted to lie here and admire them forever, his heart beating and beating and beating.

Whitney's eyes flipped open, but she didn't seem to notice that Jeremy was staring at her. She blinked twice and sat up with start, jarring him and waking Sam.

"Helicopter," she whispered. She got to her feet, her bad ankle nearly buckling beneath her, and hobbled to a more open space. "Helicopter!" she shouted. "The helicopter's back!"

Sure enough, within moments, the thrum that had been Jeremy's heartbeat had turned into a distinct *whup-whup-whup* of helicopter blades. The trees bent and swayed under the spell of its current and they could make out more than sound now—they could make out the machine itself. It hovered, low, and Jeremy was almost certain he saw someone inside pointing down at them, binoculars pressed to their eyes.

"They see us!" he called, his heart leaping so hard the words came out hoarse and raspy. "They see us!"

He lurched to where Whitney was, his snakebit leg lighting up with fire, Sam following him much more slowly. She was wiping the sleep out of her eyes, too sluggish for excitement.

"Wave!" Whitney commanded. "Wave to them!"

And they did. All three of them tossed their arms in the air and waved with all of their might. Jeremy stumbled back to the blanket and grabbed his own binoculars, while Whitney and Sam untethered the survival blanket and whipped it up and down, parachuting the silver side so that it caught and blinked in the sun. Jeremy paused waving long enough to peer through his binoculars.

Two men sat in the cockpit. Jeremy couldn't tell from their headgear who they were. But he could clearly see the one who he'd thought was looking down at him talking into a radio. He set down the radio and gave Jeremy two big thumbs-up.

Jeremy dropped the binoculars, and then dropped to his knees. "Thank you, God," he said, haggard and tearful. "Thank you. They see us. Whitney. They see us!"

Whitney fell, too, and so did Sam, wrapping their arms around each other's backs, their heads bowed so that their crowns were touching, all of them laughing, crying, breathing as one. A circle of relief and gratitude.

Chapter Twenty

It was nearly dark before they got their first squawk on the walkie. Whitney, who'd been holding it in her lap, almost dropped it in her haste to respond. Jeremy was sure that she, like he, had started to have a gut-sinking feeling of bleakness creep in with every second that went by without hearing anything. He'd started to even wonder if maybe the helicopter was a cruel dream, as vivid and wrenching as his dream about Laura. Was it possible for all three of them to dream the same thing?

Whitney pressed the button on the side of the radio. "Hello? We hear you! Do you hear us? Hello?"

There was an excruciatingly long pause, and then the walkie squawked again, this time the static carrying the tiniest mumble of a voice inside of it. Whitney laughed out loud, her sparkling eyes dancing and then brimming over with tears. Jeremy felt his own cheeks tug upward, his own eyes fill.

"We're here!" she shouted into the tiny speaker,

then dropped it in her lap again, threw her head back and shouted into the forest, "We're here!"

They spent the next half hour shouting. Jeremy turned a wary eye to the sky, afraid that the coming darkness would pause or cancel the search. Rescuers could go missing trying to find lost hikers, and they could be deemed too risky to save tonight.

But at least rescuers knew where they were. The communication over the radio was a confirmation of that. The helicopter had found them. It was just a matter of getting help to them. They had to keep yelling. He cupped his hands around his mouth and hollered.

After a while, Whitney lowered herself to the ground. She rubbed her ankle and winced, then pressed her hands into her belly.

"So hungry," she said. "I hope they bring food."

"And water," Sam said. "The rainwater tastes like dirt. And it's almost gone. I can't wait to get out of here. I'm going to hug the rescuers so hard when they get to us."

Jeremy thought he might, too.

"Sam," Jeremy said. "Can you get the pack so we're ready to go when they do get here? Neither of us is in any shape to climb that hill to the cave."

That was true, but he also wanted some time alone with Whitney. He had some things he wanted to say. No. Things he *needed* to say.

Sam grumbled as she went back up the mountain. She was getting weaker. It was more obvious than Jeremy wanted to admit.

"Is your leg bad?" Whitney asked as soon as the girl was out of earshot.

He shook his head. "I'll live. Yours?"

She chewed her bottom lip. She'd gone paler recently, Jeremy couldn't help noticing. He wasn't sure what that could mean. But he was certain that it couldn't mean anything good. "Probably going to be in a cast for a while. But it'll be fine. I'm not too worried."

Jeremy wasn't sure he believed that, but he knew that her grit was part of what made him love her. Unfortunately, it was also what made her seem so dangerous. But he'd learned that you definitely can't ward off danger by refusing to live life. Danger sometimes came to you. You could greet it lonely and afraid, or you could greet it full and expectant. Whitney was a full and expectant type of person. He wanted to be, too.

"I really admire you," he said. She looked surprised. "You never once complained about that ankle. You're pretty amazing."

She shrugged. "We had a lot bigger things to worry about."

"You saved Sam."

"You would have if I hadn't been here. You'd have found a way."

"You collected the water and you spread out the reflective blanket. You kept Sam calm."

She shook her head. "You did those—"

"Would you just…" he interrupted. "Just take the compliment? I'm trying to tell you something."

She smiled shyly. He thought he saw color rise in her pale cheeks, a good sign. "Thank you. For the compliment."

"Thank you for everything you did for us."

"You're welcome." She bit her lip and there was awkward silence between them. But then she glanced into the trees. "I saw the bird again. While we were praying. It flew from me to you. To where…you were praying, too." She pressed her lips together nervously.

He ducked his head, embarrassed. Not for his prayer, but for his time spent not praying. For the time spent blaming God for the things that had gone wrong in his life. So much had gone right—could God not be equally blamed for those? How arrogant to think that the good was man-made while the divine was only in charge of grief.

"I was moved," he said.

"It was moving," she agreed. "And I know you think it's crazy, but I'm pretty sure the woodpecker has been following me. I've been so shut off since my mom died. Afraid. I think it was telling me to open my eyes."

Jeremy knew exactly what fear she was talking about. He'd been afraid, too. Maybe the bird had been following her. Maybe it had been following *them*. Again one of those conversations seemed to be filling in the silence between them. She was thinking the same about the bird being a message they both needed to hear.

This was his chance. If he wasn't going to speak his

mind now, he may live the rest of his life never doing it. He couldn't let that happen. For him. For Sam.

He moved to Whitney, staying on his knees in front of her. He touched the back of her hand with his forefinger, trying to work out the words he needed to say. He couldn't figure out how he wanted to express his feelings, only that he wanted to do it *right*.

Even through all of this, her hands somehow managed to be soft. She flipped her hand over and shivered when his finger traced her palm. Slowly, her fingers curled around his, sending warmth between their palms. He traced, and then embraced, the other hand.

The words jumbled and bubbled together until he could no longer keep them inside. He still wasn't sure what he wanted to say; he had to trust that he would say it anyway, without overthinking.

"You asked me if I felt it, too," he said, looking deep into her eyes.

"Oh, that. I was just—"

"I do," he said, cutting her off. "I've felt it all along. On the bus, when you said you'd brought your own cupcakes to celebrate your birthday. Actually, even before that, when we were planning this trip and you were trying so hard not to laugh at the cheesy rescue films. And failing, by the way. You laughed."

Whitney let out a silent chuckle—a puff of air. Jeremy noticed that it sounded nervous. "Turns out, those films are kind of important."

He smiled with her, but he didn't want to get derailed. It had suddenly seemed so long since he started wanting her—longer than he was aware of.

"When you pulled Sam out of that hole. I knew then that I was falling for you."

Her eyes grew wide. "You did?"

He nodded. "I was too stubborn to let myself feel it. To let myself feel anything. But it's there. It always has been. I want to get out of here, but I don't want *this* to end." He squeezed her hands on the word *this*. "Does that make sense?"

Whitney nodded, her face flushed, her breathing shallow. "I don't want it to end, either. Us, I mean. I don't want us to end. I'm falling for you, too. I mean… I've already fallen." Her words were jumbled, which Jeremy found endearing. Real. She pointed to her ankle and then to his heart. "In more ways than one."

Three days ago, if someone had asked Jeremy about kissing a woman, he would have said he was way too rusty to try that again. He would have thought he'd somehow forgotten, that kissing was not at all like riding a bicycle.

But he would have been wrong.

The silent conversation that passed between them this time was clear as day. He could feel Whitney's grip tighten against him, feel her lean toward him just slightly—just enough to let him know that she was thinking the same thing he was.

And when he leaned in to meet her lips with his, all of the bad faded away completely. He wanted to go home, but in some ways he was already there.

Chapter Twenty-One

Sam saw them kiss. She let out a loud *whoop!*—the most energetic she'd been all day, Whitney couldn't help noticing—and when Whitney and Jeremy pulled apart abruptly, they saw her practically hanging out of the cave mouth, one fist victoriously pumping the air.

"It's about time!" she yelled.

"Be careful!" Whitney and Jeremy yelled at the same time.

"You're going to fall out of there and break your head open again," Jeremy said, getting up and going to her.

Whitney instantly felt his absence, which left her palms cold. But still she was warm from within. If she'd ever doubted whether or not she was in love with Jeremy, the kiss had dispatched that doubt completely. It was sweet—little more than a peck, really—and it was perfect.

She watched as Jeremy raised his arms and Sam tossed the backpack to him, which he caught. Sam crawled out of the cave, popped up in front of her dad, and looked him straight in the eye. "Seriously. It's about time. I've been waiting for you guys to do that since you pulled me out of that hole."

Jeremy and Whitney both laughed self-consciously.

"Well, I'm glad we didn't let you down," Jeremy said.

"Does this mean you're like, boyfriend and girlfriend now?" Sam asked.

Whitney and Jeremy exchanged glances again—a glance that Whitney felt all the way down to her toes. Was that what it meant? Having feelings for someone—falling for someone—usually led to dating, right? And dating to marriage. And marriage to family. Could she really see that happening with her and *Mr. No-No*? Would that make her *Mrs. No-No*? What would Cindy say? Whitney had to suppress a giggle.

She didn't want to get ahead of herself. But the vision was not the worst thing in the world, either. She thought maybe she could see herself with Jeremy for a long, long time. Maybe even forever. She was certainly open to it.

And she was pretty sure the look in Jeremy's eyes, and the chemistry behind that kiss, was saying the same thing.

"Let's just get out of here first," Jeremy said.

"But—"

"But, yes," he said, lifting Sam's chin with his forefinger. "Yes. I'm going to ask Whitney out on a date, and I hope she'll be my girlfriend. Okay?"

Sam smiled. So did Whitney.

The walkie-talkie made another noise, only this time the words behind the static were loud and clear.

"Whitney? Jeremy? Do you hear me? It's Rob."

Whitney's heart jumped into her throat. It had seemed like a lifetime since she heard Rob's voice. Instantly, tears sprang to her eyes. She lifted the radio to her mouth.

"Yes! Yes, I hear you, Rob."

There was a pause, and then, "Can you call out? We think we're close."

Whitney dropped the radio into her lap and opened her mouth to shout, but all that came out was a grateful sob. Her voice suddenly felt weak and spent, her gratitude overwhelming any other feeling she might have had. So much had happened in such a short time.

"Here!" Jeremy yelled. "We're here!"

"Okay, we think we have you," Rob said over the radio, his voice cutting out halfway through *you*. "We're going to set off a flare. Tell us if you see it."

Within seconds, a bright red ball rocketed into the sky, not far away. They all turned toward it. The red glow in the darkening sky streaked their faces.

"We see it," Whitney said, gulping down her emotion and getting back to business. "You're about half a mile away. North of us, I think?" She glanced at Jeremy for confirmation. He shrugged and she glanced toward the flare again. "Uphill. You're uphill from us."

"Got it," Rob said. "We'll flare again in a minute."

Jeremy started to chuckle.

"What?" Whitney said, the walkie-talkie frozen in the air close to her mouth. "What's so funny?"

"That is one thing I did not have in my pack," he said. "A flare gun. Imagine how quickly this would have been over if I'd had one."

"You should definitely put one in there for next time," Sam said.

"Next time!" Whitney and Jeremy said together.

"You want to do this again?" Whitney asked incredulously.

Sam shrugged. Again, she seemed more listless than Whitney wanted her to be. "I mean, not like tomorrow or anything."

"I think I've had my fill of nature for quite a while," Whitney said.

"Agreed," Jeremy said.

There was another *whump*—closer this time—and another ball of red lit up their faces, so bright it made Whitney squint. And then Whitney was sure she heard the whine of motors off in the distance, somewhere to her left.

"Yes," Whitney said into the radio, before Rob could even ask. "You're coming right toward us." She jumped up and began shouting. Jeremy got to his feet and joined her, clasping her hand in his. Soon even Sam was shouting.

Whitney's throat was dry and painful by the time Rob and two park rangers appeared. They almost looked like a mirage coming through the trees. They all wore orange vests and carried flashlights and machetes that they used to hack at the brush as they walked. Rob held a flare gun down at his side, his flashlight on a headband, a bobbing light on his forehead.

"Rob!" Whitney cried and ran to him, forgetting once again that her ankle would not allow her to run. She stumbled onto her knees, feeling grit and pebbles dig into them, but she didn't care. She got up and made her way to him as fast as she could, then hugged him tight. "I can't believe it!"

Rob wrapped his arms around her back as she dissolved into a flood of weepy gratitude. She could hear Jeremy and Sam talking to the park rangers, but she couldn't let go of Rob. He was stinky and his wild hair tickled her nose, but she didn't care. She was afraid if she released him, he would turn out to not be real. As long as she was holding on to him, he was actually there. And she knew that she was the reason for his dishevelment and was so grateful for his loyalty.

One of the rangers spoke coordinates into a walkie-talkie, and soon the sound of the motors grew louder. Whitney finally let go when a ranger offered her his canteen.

"Sam first," she said. Her mouth watered—how was that even possible?—as she listened to Sam gulp. When Sam was done, Whitney tipped the canteen to her mouth and drank deeply but made sure she saved some for Jeremy.

"Don't worry, there's more on the ATVs," the ranger said.

The motors continued coming closer.

"You're not that far off the path, really," Rob said. "But it's not the path we were on initially. You went on the harder side. Candle Peak is way over there. How did you get so far off?"

"I have no idea," Whitney said. It seemed to her like they had only walked in circles. But somehow they'd managed to walk all the way to the neighboring mountain. No wonder the walkie-talkie wouldn't work.

"The ATVs will be here soon," the ranger who had given them water said. "Do any of you need medical attention?"

"We all do," Jeremy answered, and something about hearing the words aloud made Whitney finally feel the throbbing in her ankle, full force. She lowered herself to a rock and straightened her leg out in front of her, certain that she couldn't put another ounce of weight on it. Sam came to her and sat in her lap. Whitney could feel the girl trembling. She must have felt the relief as physically as Whitney did. In its own way, rescue was terrifying.

Just not nearly as terrifying as snakes and lightning storms and falls.

Whitney was grateful for the ATVs. The thought of riding out of the forest rather than walking seemed so luxurious she could hardly wrap her head around it. She wasn't even sure she could have walked if she'd had to. It was almost as if her bones and muscles were finally giving out, now that she knew they no longer had to be there for her.

She leaned her forehead against Sam's back and squeezed her eyes shut. *Thank you, God*, she thought. *And, Mom, I know you were looking out for me, like you always do.* And then for good measure, added, *Laura, thank you, too.*

Sam turned slightly. She leaned in and whispered, "I've never been on an ATV before."

"Me, neither," Whitney whispered back.

"I'm kind of excited about it," Sam said.

Whitney smiled. *Never underestimate a child's ability to look on the bright side*, she thought. "Me, too." She didn't add that there were much easier ways to get to ride on an ATV than to be rescued on one. But she wanted to let Sam have her excitement her own way.

Jeremy continued to talk to Rob and the rangers about what they'd been through, at one point pulling up his pant leg so they could get a look at the snakebite. Under the bright light of the flashlights, the skin looked even bluer and puffier, and the men made grave noises at seeing it. Whitney was glad he would get some medical attention soon and hoped that he didn't have too many lingering problems. But she knew she would be there for him if he needed her, for as long as he needed her, the same way she knew he would be there for her if she needed him.

The sound of the motors grew louder yet and were joined by the sound of gravel and brush being moved. The buzz lulled Whitney and had she been sitting against something, or lying down, she might have even gone to sleep, her brain blissfully unaware of where she was or what she needed to do. For the first time in three days, she was able to fully let her guard down.

Soon, they were striped by the beams of headlights as four ATVs came into view. The small four-wheelers looked different with their elongated beds on the back. They reminded Whitney of tiny trucks.

The riders dismounted and turned on floodlights that bathed the entire area, like they were the stars of some horrible reality TV survival show. The riders were a blur of words and motion, Whitney's brain too tired to keep up with either. She heard something about a first aid kit, something else about water and while her brain screamed, *Yes! Yes, please! More water!* she continued to sit with her eyes closed. Stretcher, food, concussion… All words that swam around her, but never really touched her.

She opened her eyes at the scuffing of feet and saw Sam lifted off her lap by one of the rescuers. Sam wrapped her arm around the rescuer's neck and he carried her to the back of an ATV. He deposited her onto a jump seat and buckled her in.

Jeremy approached Whitney and crouched down. She noticed that he, too, was keeping one leg straighter than the other, his weight shifted away from it.

"Hey," he whispered. "You okay?"

She took in his face—really took it in—for the first time. The worry lines etched into his tanned forehead. The slim nose and piercing eyes. The way his whole face told what was going on inside of him. Worry. Care. Love. She placed a hand on his shoulder.

"I'm just tired," she said.

He held his hand over hers and nodded. "So am I. But we're about to get some real rest."

Rob approached Jeremy and patted him on the back. "Sam's all buckled in. You ready?"

Jeremy, only briefly distracted from Whitney, nodded, then turned back to her. "We'll be right there."

Rob hesitated. Whitney felt his surprise in that hesitation, and realized it was going to be a surprise that she would need to get used to. People weren't accustomed to either one of them being part of a "we."

"Okay. Sure. I've got your pack."

Jeremy grinned, his eyes never leaving Whitney's. "You can burn it." They both chuckled.

It seemed like a lifetime ago that she was encouraging him to go lighter in his pack. How many times over the past three days had she wished she hadn't done that? How many times had she wished she hadn't left hers at the rest stop. But she supposed all three of them were filled with wishes that would have changed what happened, or even kept it from happening altogether.

What then? Whitney thought. *Would you have ever realized how you felt about this man?*

Yes, she answered herself, almost without thought. *We would have found each other no matter what.* And she was certain of that.

She turned her hand so that it was holding his and then reached for his other hand, allowing him to pull her to standing. Once again, her leg wanted to buckle beneath her. Jeremy slipped an arm around her waist to steady her.

"I've got you," he said. He pulled her closer to him, and she wrapped her arm around his neck similar to the way Sam had done with the rescuer.

"Yes, you do," she whispered, but she was pretty sure he didn't hear.

He was limping on his other leg, and probably any of the other men would have been steadier traversing the uneven ground to the ATV. But this somehow seemed perfect to Whitney. Together, they lurched and limped, paused and powered on. They were broken, bruised, bleeding in so many ways. But they would prop each other up and somehow, by the grace of God, they would get through.

Chapter Twenty-Two

"You really do sing terribly," Jeremy said. He elbowed Cindy, who threw her head back and laughed.

"What didn't you like about it?" she asked, feigning innocence.

"Everything," Jeremy said. "Well, okay, maybe not everything. Just the words, the tune and the fact that you did it out loud."

This time, Cindy paired her laughter with a soft punch to the shoulder. "Thanks for clarifying. What can I say? What I lack in talent, I more than make up for in exuberance."

"That's true," Whitney said, putting her arm around her friend and giving her a side hug. "And I actually think you're getting better."

"Thank you, friend," Cindy said, aiming the heavy stress on the word *friend* at Jeremy.

He wrapped an arm around her from the other side and squeezed, too. "You know I'm just teasing you.

Think of how boring your life would be without my charming banter."

"I do. And I'll take your not-so-charming banter over not having you around any day. That was horrible. Worst three days of my life."

When the ATVs had delivered the three of them to the parking lot at the end of the long Glowing Pines trail, ambulances were waiting. Sam and Jeremy went into one, and Whitney went into the other. But just as they were about to close the door, Whitney saw Cindy running across the parking lot, yelling to hold the door.

She'd bounded into the ambulance and wrapped Whitney in the world's biggest hug. They'd both cried their eyes out. Cindy rode to the hospital with Whitney and stayed by her side the entire time. When they'd finally released Whitney, Cindy went home with her and didn't leave until the next morning. She'd slept on the floor next to Whitney's bed so she could comfort her when nightmares woke her friend.

The next morning, Whitney had sheepishly told Cindy all about the new development between her and Jeremy. She told her about the kiss, and how it had all just felt right.

She would have been lying if she said she wasn't a little worried that the romance was "all about the mountain," but after sleeping on it, she only wanted to be with Jeremy more. It felt strange to wake up without him nearby, without being able to check on Sam. Without hearing the little girl hum and talk to herself.

"You and Mr. No-No?" Cindy asked incredulously.

"Yes-yes," Whitney said, inhaling her coffee deeply before savoring the first sip. Everything seemed luxurious to her now—her mattress, fresh clothing, toast—as if she was experiencing it all for the first time. The night before, she'd taken the boot and wrap off of her ankle and stood in the steaming shower until the water turned cold. Even then, the coldness felt new and different, and she tipped her face up toward the showerhead, opening her mouth to literally drink it in. "Me and Mr. No-No. He's different than that, though. He's…well, he's amazing."

Cindy had shaken her head in disbelief but refrained from saying anything else. Ever since, Whitney noticed that Cindy had changed toward him. She seemed to really listen to him, had started teasing him. And soon they were the best of friends.

And now… Well, now they were here. Jeremy teasing Cindy about her singing.

Whitney broke away from the revelry, noticing Sam had separated herself from the group and was sitting alone, her arms wrapped around her knees. She was staring off into the distance. Whitney sat next to her.

"Hey," she said, looking out in the same direction that Sam was. Greens, oranges, reds, browns. Beautiful. "What are you doing over here by yourself?"

"Do you think that's it?" Sam asked. She lifted her finger and pointed. "The hole I fell into?"

Whitney tried to follow Sam's finger, but could see nothing but the tops of the trees. Seventh grade had been hard for Sam, who had found herself a local celebrity for reasons she definitely didn't want. She was mortified by being the kid who'd gone missing on Candle Mountain, and there was nothing middle schoolers can home in on and exploit quicker than a classmate's mortification.

Whitney and Jeremy had talked extensively about whether or not to go back up the mountain, especially on such an important day. They wavered between it being healing for Sam, or damaging her. They'd gone over it so many times, talking in circles, never coming to a conclusion. And then Sam, unaware of their angst, had suggested it herself, and it was a done deal. Up the mountain, they would go. Of course on this day. An incredibly important day.

When they'd started their hike, they'd paused at the mouth of the trail, holding hands—Whitney, Jeremy, Sam. Whitney was unprepared for the feelings it would stir inside of her.

"Okay, everybody, let's offer up a short one," Sam said in her Mister Rob voice, breaking the silence. They all chuckled and then bowed their heads. "Dear God, protect us as we go up this tiny little hill together. And help us all stay on the trail together."

"Amen!" Whitney and Jeremy shouted together. Laughter. Turned out it was just the thing that she needed to propel one foot in front of the other.

It had taken hours, but their spirits were good. Cindy and Rob and the entire youth group. Jeremy's parents had taken a shuttle to the top and would meet them there. Some of the other nurses were doing the same. They sang songs and told jokes and spent some time silently contemplating, especially as they passed the rest area. And when they finally got to the crest of Candle Peak—celebration!

Sitting next to Sam, staring at what they'd now conquered in more ways than one, Whitney could finally appreciate the beauty of the mountain. And also the humbling nature of it. "Could be the same hole, I guess," Whitney said softly.

"It's really small from up here," Sam said. "Don't you think it's weird how all that stuff is so small from up here, but when you're down there in it, it's so huge you might actually die?"

Whitney thought about it. She was pretty sure that Sam just described… Well, everything. What seems insurmountable while you're in its grip becomes small with a shift in perspective. Even love. The kind that used to terrify Whitney. The kind of love where you tell each other *I love you* every single day. The kind of love she and Jeremy had found. "Really weird," she agreed. "But you know that's never going to happen again, right?"

"Yeah. I know," Sam said on a sigh. "But I also don't want to forget that it did happen. Like, it's part of me, even if I don't want it to be. Does that make sense?"

Whitney nodded. Sam was so much wiser than she even knew. It was because of this wisdom that both Whitney and Jeremy knew she would make it through everything just fine. "Trust me, I don't think any of us will ever forget. Personally, I'm glad it happened."

Sam tore her eyes away from the forest and turned her gaze to Whitney. "You're *glad*?"

"Sure," Whitney said. "Getting lost in those woods brought us together. It's one of the best things that has ever happened in my life."

Sam chewed on her lip as she absorbed this. "True," she finally said. "Mine, too."

They sat for a while in silence, and then Whitney stood, brushing off the seat of her pants. Cindy had insisted she wear white cargo shorts and a white shirt, no matter how impractical for hiking. She held out a hand for Sam. "Come on. We should join the others."

Sam took Whitney's hand, and they trotted back to the party. Cindy had already laid out the food on the small camping table Jeremy's parents had brought and decorated with a white tablecloth, white and green bells. The cupcakes were white on white, with a deep green glitter sprinkled into the icing, and luscious lemon curd inside. They sparkled in the late afternoon sunlight. So did Sam, her hair still pinned and glittered from the reception the night before, a sharp contrast to her hiking gear. Pushed together in a clump as they were, Whitney could smell sunscreen and sweat.

Whitney and Jeremy each picked up a cupcake. They smirked at each other and then went for the smash, shoving cupcake into each other's mouths, maybe the only traditional part in this whole process. The crowd cheered. Cindy picked up a cupcake and held it high over her head.

"To the bride and groom!" she crowed, and again everyone cheered, including Whitney and Jeremy. And, loudest of all, Sam. "May you enjoy a lifetime at the *peak* of happiness! Huh? Huh?" She wiggled her eyebrows while everyone groaned.

Whitney used her thumb to wipe icing from around Jeremy's mouth and he did the same around hers.

"Everything good?" he asked, nodding toward Sam, who was busy devouring her second cupcake already.

"Yeah, I think so," Whitney said. "Actually, I know so. Better than good." She leaned in and wrapped her arms around him, inhaling his familiar scent of aftershave, which still clung to him even after a day of hiking. "Everything's great."

He jumped. "Oh! I almost forgot. I have one more thing."

He pulled himself away from Whitney and jogged to his backpack, which he'd propped against a nearby rock, then took it farther away from the crowd. He unzipped the pack and retrieved something from it, then lifted his hand to the sky. "For the woman who rescued me!" he yelled. The crowd quieted, curious. "I love you, Mrs. Whitney Moon."

"What is that?" Cindy whispered.

Whitney was laughing too hard to answer. Jeremy squeezed his finger, and there was a loud pop. A ball of light—dimmed by the sun—sailed into the sky.

"A flare!" Sam said, beaming at her dad. "He remembered!"

"It's perfect. Absolutely perfect," Whitney said, wiping her eyes with one hand while pulling her new stepdaughter to her side with the other. "I love you, too."

Epilogue

The sun was just coming up when Whitney's alarm went off, pulling her out of a familiar dream about lemon cheesecake. It was her birthday; her third without her mother. She'd taken a vacation day, but she wanted to get an early start. She had big plans with Sam. Pancakes, followed by shopping, noodles for lunch at a trendy fusion restaurant, more shopping, an iced tea, and head home for dinner and cake. Not lemon cheesecake. That was her mom's thing. Chocolate cake with chocolate frosting was Sam's favorite, and even though it was Whitney's birthday, she liked the idea of Sam's favorite being "her thing." The same way Sam had embraced "Laura's thing" during her ninth birthday.

Whitney wrapped herself in her fuzzy robe, grabbed a cup of coffee, inhaled deeply, and then stuffed her feet into slippers. She left the coffee on the kitchen table to cool and headed to the shed out back, the dew on the grass licking her ankles and dampening the toes of her slippers.

The door to the shed always stuck, so she yanked on it extra hard, and it popped open, nearly throwing her onto her backside. But she caught herself and squinted into the shadows. The sun was still behind the shed, making it hard to see inside. Fortunately, she knew the shed like the back of her hand.

Inside was tidy, now that summer was on its way out—a cleared-off gardener's table, various hibernating lawn instruments, a still-inflated tube for float trips, bags of dirt and fertilizer and grass seed. And, in the corner, a stack of containers. She went to those, her slippers scuffing against the concrete floor.

Black oil sunflower seeds, raisins, cracked corn and a stack of suet cakes. She grabbed an empty basket from the gardener's table and began filling it with the containers, being sure to include a scoop.

When they'd finished their prayer just prior to their rescue from Candle Mountain, the woodpecker had flown away. Whitney had remained vigilant ever since, hoping to get a chance to thank it for what it had done for her. But she'd never seen it again.

After they married, Jeremy surprised Whitney by buying and building her a variety of bird feeders and houses and hanging them all over the backyard. Most days, Whitney delighted in the antics of the squirrels, the tiny whistling trill of the cedar waxwings, and the short, fat bodies of the Carolina wrens. But though she watched and waited, sometimes for hours on end, no woodpeckers ever showed.

She'd done her research on how to attract wood-peckers. She hung suet cakes like holiday ornaments and faithfully kept the hummingbird feeders filled. She put out raisins and barrels' worth of black oil sunflower seeds. She even coaxed Jeremy into leaving behind a snag when one of the oak trees snapped during a heavy storm, in hopes that the dying stump left behind might make the yard even more enticing.

But nothing.

As the sun continued to rise, the birds singing themselves awake and the feeling of morning movement in the air, Whitney drifted from feeder to feeder, filling each one. As per ritual, she talked to the birds while she fed them, telling each of them that she hoped they had a good day, and if they knew her woodpecker friend, please tell him that she says hello.

She'd just finished filling her last feeder when she heard a familiar laughing call, as if someone had just told the best birdy joke in the world.

Her head snapped up.

On the limb directly above her sat a woodpecker. *The* woodpecker? It was so close, she thought she might be able to see herself reflected in its eyes.

"Oh," she said, putting her hand to her chest, nearly unable to believe what she was seeing. It wasn't a question—this was the same woodpecker that had led her around the mountain. She just knew it. "It's you. Where have you been?"

The bird hopped toward the tree trunk and then back toward her. It squatted and rose, turning its head this way and that, eliciting a laugh out of Whitney. It looked like it was dancing.

"I've brought you some food," she said. "Delicious suet. Be patient." She paused, glancing around the yard, feeling a little silly—not for talking to a bird, but for what she was about to say. She leaned in and lowered her voice conspiratorially. "I married him, you know."

The bird hopped, twitched, did its nervous bird thing.

"So thank you."

She watched as the bird flew to a different branch and regarded her from another angle. Then to another, and another. The sun had come up completely. Birds were happily flitting to the feeders on the far side of the yard. The next-door neighbor's cocker spaniel had come outside to bark a good morning to the world. The grass blades showed off their dewy jewelry before the sun burned it off for the day. The air was crisp and smelled good. Funnily enough, a storm was waiting in the wings, poised to push through just after dusk.

Whitney was brought back to her excitement that day of their first trip up Glowing Pines Trail. She thought about something Jeremy had said to her on the bus, during that first, awkward conversation.

"Wow, you're really nothing but excited about this, aren't you?"

It wasn't accusatory, even though he'd already made it abundantly clear that he was not excited in the least. He'd said it with something more like awe in his voice, as if he plainly couldn't imagine being so happy.

Little did he know, at the time, how much of her excitement was manufactured. He had no idea the pain she'd been in, how deeply she felt her loss, how determined she was to never feel that hurt again.

"How much has changed since then," she found herself saying aloud to the bird, which had landed on a closer branch again and was now eyeing the suet feeder. She knew it was silly, but she felt like she was talking to her mom, a gut feeling that she'd experienced the first time she ever saw the bird. "I've got love. And it's scary. But it's also wonderful. Really, really wonderful. Even though I know it could end." She swallowed, images of Jeremy's potential demise, of Sam's, trying to force their way in. She couldn't help thinking about those things, that one day she could lose one or even both of them. It would crush her.

She glanced over at the swing set that Sam was too old for now, but that she would occasionally still go to when she'd had a particularly rough day. On those days, Whitney would join her stepdaughter, usually with a peanut butter and jelly sandwich and glass of milk. She would sit on the swing next to Sam's and silently watch the world until Sam was ready to talk. Sometimes they would talk until dinnertime had passed and Whitney was forced to order a pizza. Then they would sit at the kitchen table and talk over the pizza.

"I used to think it wasn't worth it to put that kind of trust in a relationship, but I was wrong. Every day—including the bad days—I know that even if I had to give it up, I would still want to have had it. It is so worth it."

Her hand twitched, wanting to reach out to the woodpecker. A silly part of her thought it might let her touch her fingers to its red cap. Might let her stroke its feathers. But the spell was broken when the back door opened and Jeremy stepped out onto the deck, holding a coffee cup in each hand.

"Good morning!" He held up her cup. "I poured you a fresh one. Yours got cold."

Whitney smiled. What a dear man Jeremy was.

He sipped from his cup, then nodded toward the feeder next to Whitney. "The birds are sure happy this morning."

She turned back to her bird, but it was gone. The branch bare. She scanned all of the branches she could see, but they, too, were empty. Gone. As if it had never been there.

But as Whitney bent to pick up her basket, a cool breeze ruffling her sleep-messed hair, she didn't feel desperation. She didn't feel sadness. She felt excitement and love. She had a sense that she'd said what needed to be said. To herself, to the bird, to her mother, to the universe, to God. The bird didn't cause these things to happen; he'd only allowed her to see it.

Or, who knew, maybe she would have seen it all by herself. In the end, did it really even matter?

"Be right there!" she called.

She carried the basket back to the shed and hurried to put things away. She no longer worried about whether or not the bird was real. It didn't matter, because the memories of her mother were real. The love she felt for Jeremy and Sam was real.

She shut the shed door and crossed the lawn toward Jeremy. She would keep today's woodpecker visit to herself. A sweet little gift that only she knew about.

"Success with the suet?" he asked, just like he often did.

She shrugged. "Who knows for sure?"

"Just keep putting it out there. Eventually it'll work."

She took the coffee from him and sipped. He held his arm out and she ducked under it, allowing him to rest it around her shoulders. He'd just said what she planned to live by for the rest of her life. *Keep putting it out there... Skin in the game.*

"Happy birthday, by the way," he said. "I've got party hats for later."

Whitney laughed and let Jeremy lead her toward the door. He slid it open and stepped through. But just before Whitney followed him inside, she heard telltale knocking from the oak where she'd last seen the woodpecker.

Tap-tap-tap.

She smiled. *Back atcha, my friend.*

She stepped inside, turned, took a deep breath of

sweet fall air that filled her to the tips of her toes and closed the door.

It was her birthday. She had so much to celebrate.

* * * * *

LOVE INSPIRED

Stories to uplift and inspire

Fall in love with Love Inspired—
inspirational and uplifting stories of faith
and hope. Find strength and comfort in
the bonds of friendship and community.
Revel in the warmth of possibility and the
promise of new beginnings.

Sign up for the Love Inspired newsletter
at **LoveInspired.com** to be the first
to find out about upcoming titles,
special promotions and exclusive content.

CONNECT WITH US AT:

Facebook.com/LoveInspiredBooks

Twitter.com/LoveInspiredBks

Katherine placed a hand on his shoulder. "Don't move," she said.

He blinked and she caught a glimpse of sapphire-blue eyes. He let out another groan.

"Just stay still and let me look at your head."

"I'm fine." He rolled to his side and he squinted up at her. "Who're you?"

"I'm Dr. Katherine Gilroy, so I think I'm the better judge of whether or not you're fine. You have a head wound, which means possible concussion." She reached for him. "What's your name?"

He pushed her hand away. "Dominic O'Ryan. A branch caught me. Knocked me loopy for a few seconds, but not out. We were running from the shooter." His eyes sharpened. "He's still out there." His hand went to his right hip, gripping the empty holster next to the badge on his belt. A star within a circle. "Where's my gun? Where's Carl? My partner, Carl Manning. We need to get out of here."

"I'm sorry," Katherine said, her voice soft. "He didn't make it."

He froze. Then horror sent his eyes wide—and searching. They found the man behind her and Dominic shuddered.

After a few seconds, he let out a low cry, then sucked in another deep breath and composed his features. The intense moment lasted only a few seconds, but Katherine knew he was compartmentalizing, stuffing his emotions into a place he could hold them and deal with them later.

She knew because she'd often done the same thing. Still did on occasion.

In spite of that, his grief was palpable, and Katherine's heart thudded with sympathy for him. She moved back to give him some privacy, her eyes sweeping the hills around them once more. Again, she saw nothing, but the hairs on the back of her neck were standing straight up. "I think we need to find some better cover."

As if to prove her point, another crack sounded. Katherine grabbed the first-aid kit with one hand and pulled Dominic to his feet with the other. "Run!"

Don't miss
Mountain Fugitive *by Lynette Eason,*
available October 2021 wherever
Love Inspired Suspense books and ebooks are sold.

LoveInspired.com

IF YOU ENJOYED THIS BOOK, DON'T MISS NEW EXTENDED-LENGTH NOVELS FROM LOVE INSPIRED!

In addition to the Love Inspired books you know and love, we're excited to introduce even more uplifting stories in a longer format, with more inspiring fresh starts and page-turning thrills!

Stories to uplift and inspire.

Fall in love with Love Inspired—inspirational and uplifting stories of faith and hope. Find strength and comfort in the bonds of friendship and community. Revel in the warmth of possibility, and the promise of new beginnings.

LOOK FOR THESE LOVE INSPIRED TITLES ONLINE AND IN THE BOOK DEPARTMENT OF YOUR FAVORITE RETAILER!

LITRADE0921